PLAYED

an Elite PR novel

CLARE JAMES

Entangled Publishing, LLC
2614 South Timberline Road
Suite 109
Fort Collins, CO 80525
Visit our website at www.entangledpublishing.com.

Brazen is an imprint of Entangled Publishing, LLC. For more information on our titles, visit www.brazenbooks.com.

Edited by Vanessa Mitchell
Cover design by Heather Howland
Cover art from iStock

Manufactured in the United States of America

First Edition October 2015

ENTANGLED
BRAZEN

"I'll go home. And I'll think of some way to get him back. After all…tomorrow is another day."
— *Scarlett O'Hara*

Chapter One

I need to see you.

Melody Sharp read the subject line on the email and shivered in her pale blue Lilly Pulitzer. Her skin turned downright icy—no easy feat in Atlanta in August—so she covered her goose-pimpled arms with the cardigan that draped over her office chair.

How did he find her?

A familiar ache throbbed inside her chest. It'd happened so long ago, but that pain of rejection remained close to the surface. It hit her so hard, she thought she might lose her lunch, and that pissed her right off. It was beyond mortifying that five little words on the computer screen could send her into such a tizzy.

If she were at home, she'd break something. A bunch of somethings. But that was out of the question, as she sat in the fishbowl of a cubical she'd been exiled to after her recent demotion. She knew her boss's spies were watching her as she'd slunk inside the Elite Public Relations office doors well past eight a.m., and she knew they were watching her now. Especially her nemesis, who she had affectionately named The Weasel.

Her lackadaisical attitude was to blame, but she couldn't help it. She just wasn't feeling it anymore. What was once a fun and challenging career had turned into a chore. Ugh, adulting. Even at twenty-five, Mel was far from mastering it. So she'd been avoiding everything, pretending her craphole of a life belonged to someone else. Of course, deep down she knew it was ridiculous to fight the inevitable, and it was *so* past time to grow up. But why bother when she really had no idea what she wanted to do with her life?

Then the ominous email arrived.

Not the message I was looking for, Universe.

Without a thought to what she was doing, she began ripping her brown paper bag into tiny little pieces, stacking them in neat piles next to her keyboard. Lovely. Like she needed to call any more attention to her current mental state. She quickly brushed the paper aside, grabbed the stress ball off her desk, and squeezed. Typically, she used it to pelt the interns in the head when they annoyed her, so it was kind of nice to actually handle it for its intended purpose for a change.

Mel never really had the need for a stress ball before. Before the demotion, she occupied a spacious office—with real walls—on the east side of the building, which overlooked Peachtree Street downtown. A perfectly acceptable place to have a breakdown. In private. But that was back before she lost her way. Before her best friend moved to North Carolina and left her to contend with her boss, Miranda Wells, aka the

Ice Queen, on her own, and before she slid into her quarter-life crisis (yes, it was really a thing!) and began effing up her life royally.

After Mel's third or fourth misstep, Miranda threw down the gauntlet, saying if Mel was going to contribute like an entry-level employee, then she'd be treated as such. And that meant the office space of a peon, with a salary to match.

Mel wasn't quite sure which was worse.

She took a long, fortifying breath to steady her nerves and get her anger in check but instead gagged a little. One of her new cubical mates brought the most putrid smelling dish to his desk—some fish and egg combo that was so offensive the entire staff of interns shifted in their seats.

"Sorry, dudes." The lunch offender responded to the gasps and complaints now roaring behind the maze of partitions. "I'm on a strict protein diet."

Good Lord, it was college all over again. On a normal day, Mel would join them and set the kid straight. However, this afternoon had been anything but normal, and there were more pressing issues to deal with. She huddled closer to her laptop and checked the email again, just to be sure her eyes weren't playing tricks on her.

I need to see you.

It wasn't so much the subject line that had chilled her blood as it was the name on return email address: Teddy McBride. The *dot-de* instead of *dot-com* told her he was contacting her from Germany. The place he'd fled to three years ago.

She could conjure up the memory of that day so easily. Her wound was still tender; it had never healed quite right. Looking back, it reminded her of the ending of *Gone with*

the Wind, when she cried and begged her very own Rhett
Butler to stay. Told him she couldn't live without him. But
all he could say was, "Frankly my dear, I don't give a damn,"
before he walked off into the sunset. Okay, it was probably
more along the lines of, "Sorry, baby," with a peck on the
cheek as he left the Sweetwater Country Club, but Mel
appreciated theatrics.

She had always wanted to be Scarlett O'Hara, uncon-
ventional and brave, a woman who made her own rules. Unfortunately, she ended up coming off more like Celia Foote
from *The Help*—a pretty, ditsy caricature of a woman who
was about as smart as tree bark. Which explained why she
never saw it coming. Yes, Melody's door to happiness didn't
so much close as slam in her face. No warning. No apology.
Just one big FU and a kick to her fine china.

Instead of the proposal she was expecting, her boyfriend
of six years had informed her that he was going to graduate
school in Dusseldorf…in front of the whole damn town. Or
over lunch in the Willow Room, same difference. Anyone
who was anyone in Sweetwater had been there that day, and
those who weren't heard about it soon enough. It was the
small town way.

Teddy said he wasn't ready to settle down. He wanted to
meet new people and experience new things. He wanted an
adventure. All code for: she was boring and inexperienced…
and not enough for him.

Her entire world came crumbling down with his admission. One minute she was preparing for the wedding of the
decade, the next she was skipping town in the middle of the
night. That was how she'd arrived in Atlanta. She moved to
the city to get away from it all, to save face. But mostly she

relocated in a desperate attempt to win back the douchebag. She thought if she left Sweetwater and became some sophisticated city girl, he'd find her so irresistible, he'd beg her to come back to him. Yeah, that never happened.

Now, from a flipping ocean away, Teddy McBride still had an unyielding power over her—even after all this time—and that really dilled her pickle.

I need to see you.

Her fingers hovered over the mouse. Should she open it?

She jumped when her phone buzzed. "Shit."

Miranda.

"Bring in your notes from the Falcons meeting," Miranda barked, snapping her out of her painful reverie.

"Right away, ma'am," she said, biting her lip to hold back all the other responses that threated to escape. Elite—a PR firm of spin doctors and publicists for the rich and famous— was handling the kickoff to the football season. It was one of their biggest events and one Mel should've taken a lead role in. Instead, she was tasked with recording the minutes at all of the status meetings.

She hung up with Miranda and flipped her phone the bird. The intern sitting in the cubical across from her giggled. She was one of the only people Mel could impress these days.

Trudging through Intern's Row, Mel still couldn't believe that she now officed there—amid a mishmash of college kids with tiny headphones in their ears and giant cans of Monster on their desks. She glared at Smelly Lunch Guy, who quickly dropped his head to brace for an ass-whooping. She didn't have the time or energy to give him one.

Her boss played for blood, she'd give her that. The entire situation was beyond humiliating, but Mel wasn't about to let it break her. Not yet. Once she reached the designated *Events* area, where she'd once belonged, she painted on her game face and charged ahead toward the executive suite. Her colleagues pretended not to see her. *Traitorous assholes.*

"Here you are." She approached Miranda's desk with the paperwork after the requisite three knocks outside her door. Her boss preferred to have the notes printed out so she could page through them while she ran on her treadmill in the evenings. Yes, Miranda lived to work, and expected everyone else to do the same. The woman was a force of nature, and everything about her was severe, intense, and colder than a polar bear's butt. No one would deny she was gorgeous—with dark, shoulder-length hair, the bluest eyes you'd ever seen, and just as thin as could be. She was also scary as hell.

"Next time"—she flipped through the notes without giving Mel even a single icy glance—"let's be proactive, so I don't have to hound you for such simple material."

"Mmm-hmm." Mel said, afraid to open her mouth any further. She was already rattled and raw, and so close to telling the Ice Queen where she could shove that *simple material.*

"And don't forget the seminar on Wednesday," Miranda added, turning her back in dismissal. "Frankie Fink has words to live by."

As if she could forget. The Women in Business seminars were another requirement of Mel's probation. But hey, at least she'd get away from the interns for the day. She had to stay positive, and just hang on until Labor Day—four weeks away. That's when she'd be forced to go back to Sweetwater for the town's *Last Hurrah of Summer* celebration. She made it back every year—her mama and daddy would be devastated if she didn't. Mostly though, her attendance was all part of her own personal PR campaign and reputation management. She had to show the good people of Sweetwater just how fabulous her life was…without Teddy. So returning home *sans* her fancy job wasn't an option, especially after hearing from the town's golden boy. That only made her want to prove herself more.

But she had nothing to prove to *him*. So no, she would not open his email. As far as she was concerned, it never happened. Dang, she was good at denial. At least that was something.

Back in her cube, Mel finished compiling the Falcons' media kit and social media pages for the event—things she hadn't done since her first year under Miranda's thumb. She shut down her email window so she wouldn't be tempted by Teddy's note. Though it didn't stop her finger from itchin'.

What would he possibly have to say to her after all this time?

She waited until all her work was done for the day before she pulled up her email again, unable to stop herself from scrolling back to Teddy McBride and his stupid *dot-de* address.

I need to see you.

The words had played on a loop in her head the entire day and she couldn't take it another second. So she placed a finger to her mouse. And then opened it.

I am not a slut. I am not a slut. I am not a slut.

Twelve hours later, Mel beat herself up as she made the last leg of her *literal* walk of shame back to her apartment. The normally lively street in her trendy neighborhood was finally asleep, though the remnants of its wild nightlife remained scattered all over the pavement—cigarette butts here, beer bottles there, condom wrappers along the curbside, alleyways full of trash.

This party hotspot had been rode hard and put away wet.

Much like she felt.

Of course, Mel was a modern woman and so not into slut shaming. Still…she was walking the streets at five a.m. With her panties in her purse!

Hey, at least she got her undies back. Because Lord knows what some creepers would do with them. She'd just read an article about girls selling their unmentionables to make a few bucks—used panties were apparently in high demand, now worth more money online than breast milk. And if Mel didn't get her shit together soon, she'd have to sell both just to make rent.

So things weren't exactly going as planned lately…but nobody could call her boring anymore. It may have taken her three years to do something wild and crazy, but she finally did it. Who cares if she knew the guy? Or that he was her friend? The point was, boring and inexperienced women didn't hook up on a weekday night.

Boom! Take that, Teddy.

Ow. She couldn't go there right now. Not with her gray matter throbbing in her head, or the acid rolling in her stomach. No, she refused to acknowledge that maybe, just maybe, that one pesky email from Teddy proclaiming that he had to "see her" may have been the bee sting to her ass that prompted her very first one-night stand. Not like Mel was celibate or anything, she just preferred to be dating for a few weeks before she became on a first name basis with a penis. But the little blast from the past shot that standard to hell.

I need to see you.

She must've read that line a hundred times before opening it. It wasn't all it said.

Dear Mel,

I'm coming home. I'll be back the day before the Last Hurrah.

Meet me at our spot before the parade? It's important.

T.M

Well, what could she say? After reading the cryptic email from her ex, she panicked…and had a few too many tequila shots to take the edge off. Next thing she knew, she was tangled under the sheets with her friend.

Kevin Wallis worked in her building downtown and lived only a few blocks away. Lucky for her. By day, he was an investment banker. By night, he ran a crazy successful blog about the nightlife in Atlanta. She met him her first week in the city, during lunch, and they hit it off right away. He was smart, hot, and totally connected—the perfect person to give her a taste of what she came to Atlanta for. Though she had never really taken him up on it. Until last night. And now, he had truly given her everything.

Not that anyone would know what she'd been up to. She looked perfectly composed in her sundress and sandals. Her makeup was flawless. That was no accident—she'd stopped in Kevin's bathroom and freshened up before she left. Just because she was acting like a harlot, didn't mean she had to look like one. She was a Southern lady, after all. Well, mostly…

Shit, her feet ached. She stopped to release the buckle on the damn sandals, desperately wishing she'd worn her sneakers. She tried for the next best thing and let the straps flop around her ankles as she walked the last block home. Just a few more measly yards and she could get a couple of hours of sleep before she had to leave for work.

Mel dodged what might have been a puddle of pee on the side of the road, making a little jump over the curb. She'd gone looking for an adventure last night. This wasn't what she had in mind, but at least she was out there experiencing new things.

Had *he* done the same?

She wasn't so naive as to think that, after three years abroad, Teddy hadn't sampled the local cuisine. Really, she didn't care if he had. Even though hearing from him out of the blue struck a nerve, she'd been over him for a long time now. Of course, those first few months had been excruciating. She had cried herself to sleep every night, called home every day, and checked her phone incessantly, praying he'd call. It went on that way for so long it'd become normal, until Miranda hired her. Once she joined the Elite team, there wasn't time for any sort of wallowing.

Really, with the exception of her lack of judgment last night, she had made a good life for herself alone in the city. Mel hadn't known a single soul in Atlanta when she'd moved that summer after college graduation. Her apartment in Little Five Points—a bohemian area of the city that was about as far from her hometown of Sweetwater as you could get—had been her humble abode for three years now. True, she stuck out like a sore thumb with her preppy clothes and bright colors amidst the dark hipster-wear of the area, but she loved it here.

It was a place known for its restaurants, bars, and shops, but at the ass crack of dawn, you'd never know it. Except for the stench. The pungent stink of stale beer and quite possibly vomit made her own stomach turn. She needed to move fast or she'd find herself hurling on the side of the road like a freshman during rush week.

Finally, she rounded the corner to her place—an older home that'd been converted into three apartments. A place she might not have for much longer unless she seriously turned things around. The pale yellow house stood proud on the corner with its wrap-around porch. It was that porch, with its colorful Adirondack chairs, that had captivated Mel initially. She envisioned hanging out there after work and having cocktails with friends, kicking back on those chairs on a hot evening while reading a book, even serving sweet tea to her parents when they came up to visit.

Two out of three wasn't so bad.

She couldn't blame her parents; they had the business to take care of. Not to mention her sisters (and their families) were all in Sweetwater, so there wasn't much need to leave. Strange how things turned out. Who would've ever thought that Mel would be the one to move to the city and land the big job? Or be the last to get a ring on her finger?

She was so focused on that depressing thought that she didn't notice the moving truck parked in front of the house. So when she opened the door that led to her apartment, she wasn't exactly expecting to see a guy dragging a mattress up the stairs.

"What in the ever-loving hell?" she screamed, stumbling back into the door. Her mind flipped from one scenario to another to explain the scene in front of her. Thief? Squatter? Deliveryman?

"Oh, hey there," a deep voice said from behind the puffy white Select Comfort on the flight of stairs above. "Don't mind me. I'm just moving in."

"Just moving in?" she mocked. Meanwhile, there went ten years off her pathetic life. She didn't like being caught off guard, and she definitely didn't like surprises. It only made her ornery. Combine that with her current state of exhaustion and Mel didn't exactly show well.

She couldn't get a good look at the guy. He was hidden in the darkened hallway, but the door across from her upstairs apartment was propped open. Shit. He must be her new neighbor. She might've known that if she answered any of her landlord's calls. But she had her reasons for avoiding him.

Still, who moved at this time of day, unless you were running from the law or a woman? Either way, she didn't need the drama so close to her own living quarters when she had her own mess to deal with.

"A little early for moving day, wouldn't you say?" she snapped.

"And a little late to be coming home"—he peeked around the mattress—"dressed like *that*, wouldn't you agree?" His voice was smooth, low but clear, almost musical. She ignored what the sound did to her insides and absorbed his words instead—his condescending and judgmental words.

"Daddy, is that you?" she sing-songed. Who did he think

he was, talking down to her? She had enough of that at work. She certainly didn't have to put up with it at home, too.

"Barking up the wrong tree, little lady," he said with a smile in his voice, not letting her stop him from his work. "Not really into role-play."

Hmm, role-play. Now that could be something to explore. Somewhere between shots four and five last night, Mel decided that she was going to try this *adulting* thing—for real this time. She was on a mission to make a life here and to finally have the adventure she left home for. And whether she decided to meet Teddy or not, she'd return to Sweetwater this year a new woman. She was ready to embrace her inner Scarlett and live a life without regret.

"It's okay," her new neighbor said, interrupting her dramatic internal monologue. Heck, she was just about ready to break into song. "Whatever floats your boat, hon. I'm not here to judge."

Right. He was still talking role-play. She didn't bother to acknowledge him. Instead, she walked up the flight of stairs, squeezing against the wall of the hallway to slip past the mattress. She was not going to let this inconsiderate a-hole keep her from—she checked her watch—the hour and fifty minutes she had left for sleep. She had the world to conquer in the morning.

In front of her door at the top of the landing, she reached into her bag for the keys. But as she did, her panties fell out of her purse. Not yet accustomed to her new adventurous side, she completely forgot they were in there. Shit, this was not the first impression she wanted to make with her new housemate.

Maybe he didn't see.

She quickly bent down to grab her underwear, not daring to look back, but the man's amused chuckle told her all she needed to know. He was definitely a witness to her little humiliation.

"Not what it looks like," she lied, finally pulling her keys from the bag. She squared her shoulders and, despite the ticking clock, she took her time with the lock. She would not be shamed for...okay, yes, it *was* called the walk of shame for a reason. Still, she wouldn't be humiliated for her choices. Damn it.

"Whatever you say, princess," he said. "It's no crime." And for a brief second, she wanted to turn around. One, to see who this velvety voice belonged to, and two, to give him one of her death glares.

She resisted, opened her door, and let it slam behind her. Maybe not what Scarlett would do, but she needed her sleep first. Yes, sleep. Then she'd make her mark on the world.

And she had just four weeks to do it.

Chapter Two

*Sometimes I am two people. Johnny is the nice one. Cash
causes all the trouble. They fight.*
—Johnny Cash

Aaron Major often felt like his idol—with two distinct
personalities battling for control. There was the normal guy—the family-loving, church-going, dog-petting man
who'd lend a hand whenever he could. And then there was
the star—the egotistical, attention-seeking, skirt-chasing,
whiskey-drinking asshole who didn't give two shits about
anyone other than himself.

Though his star had fallen quite some time ago, he could
feel remnants of the guy he used to be lurking beneath his
skin, waiting to come out and play. His new neighbor was
exactly the kind of woman who provoked that guy. And she
was exactly what Aaron Major was trying to stay away from:
temptation…and things that fucked with his head in general.

That sexy Southern belle was guilty of both offenses.

He hefted another box up the flight of stairs, but her scent in the hallway was enough to do him in. Spicy, floral, and something else that filled his head with filthy thoughts. He could write an entire album about her scent.

Their little meeting in the hallway was a teaser, and he wanted more. A nice long look. But that wasn't going to happen. He wasn't going down that road again.

With only a few things left in the truck, he'd simply have to power through it. And then? Take a cold shower.

What should've taken him a handful of trips, he managed in two. So by the time he finished and dropped to the couch in his new living room, he was moments away from a heart attack. His chest ached and each breath was labored, painful to release, making his head spin. All because of a woman.

Not fucking normal, Major. Now pull it together.

He took stock of his new place: recently remodeled, with high ceilings and beautiful chestnut woodwork. It already felt like home. It may have been quite a step down from where he'd once been, but it was a step up from his last place. And that felt like the perfect position to be in, considering.

He arranged his living room, happy he found some guys to help haul in the heavy stuff the night before, all for the bargain price of a case of beer. He mounted his flat screen and shuffled a few boxes around, until he located the one marked "bathroom." Pulling out the essentials—towels, soap, and the like—he went into the shower to take care of business. And by business, he meant his aching cock.

Mercy, he'd tried to play it cool with her, but once he stole a peek at the sassy blonde who came storming into his new home, that primal need he'd kept buried for so long came rushing back. And it was like he never left Tennessee. Never mind Vegas, Nashville's the place they should call *Sin City*. A city with so much talent, so much raw energy, so many beautiful people…well, it made the freewheeling sex inevitable for a kid with a record contract.

After his early morning run-in with the temptress, he couldn't deny there was a part of him that missed it. Long, lean, and pissed as hell, she was irresistible. One of those girls who looked all prim in public, but get her out of that sorority getup and she'd have something wicked on underneath. He knew it.

Forget playing to standing-room-only auditoriums, adoring fans screaming his name, and all-night drunken benders—this girl made that shit look boring. Thank Christ he'd had a mattress to conceal his reaction to her. Especially once those lace panties came a-tumblin' from her purse.

Where'd she been when his life was also full of wild nights of debauchery? Oh, the fun they could've had. Too bad that time was long gone for him. He'd just have to stay away from her as much as possible. It had taken him over seven years to get his life back on track, and he wasn't about to let it go to shit because of a hot piece of ass.

He was determined.

Once he relieved his stress and put himself back together, he left the building to return the U-Haul—not wanting to run into his naughty neighbor until he worked up a little immunity.

That evening, Aaron vowed to keep to himself and stay clear of the siren next door. But hell if he couldn't help but take a peek out his bedroom window when he heard a car drive into the back alley. It was an unusually cool night—eighty degrees was brisk for Hotlanta—so he had the windows open to air out the stuffy apartment, which was precisely why he couldn't miss her. The squealing tires echoed through his place the second they hit the drive.

She drove a little green hybrid that he hoped wouldn't dent his pickup as it barreled into the garage. He had to hand it to the woman. She knew how to make an entrance. As she stepped out of the garage, Aaron ducked away from the window. He didn't need her thinking he was some fucking pervert watching her every move.

What was it about her that got him so worked up?

It didn't matter. He had more important things to think about, like finishing the rest of his album. So he went to work…pacing the living room, doing push-ups, searching for a word to rhyme with *fence*, watching the Braves for an inning (or three), before finally falling asleep on the couch. So, the usual.

He slept on and off, waking every few hours to contemplate his next move. He desperately wanted to create music on his own this time, but it wasn't working, and his deadline was just a few weeks away. He needed to have a completed album in less than a month, and he was still a handful of songs short.

He knew the surefire way to lay down the tracks, but it was a last resort. He wouldn't call in reinforcements unless he absolutely had to. For now, he'd try to be patient and let the creative juices flow when they were ready. Sometimes if he forced the issue, it only made matters worse.

It was a restless night, but the next time he woke up, he had something. A tune. He didn't think twice before picking up his guitar in the middle of the night. Or working a drum beat on his new coffee table. When the muse came to call, you'd better answer. He'd learned the hard way to never turn his back on the finicky bitch.

"Darlin'," came his neighbor's clipped tone from outside his door. Oh shit. He checked the time on his cable box. Five a.m. Still, he couldn't help but smile at the way she made such a sweet endearment sound like a ball-busting threat. "If you don't shut the hell up in there, I'm going to help you out." She pounded on his wall for effect. "Turn down the blasted music."

"Sorry, hon, I can't do that," he yelled back, deciding to toy with her for no reason but the fun of it. He was downright giddy that he had the hook for a new song and part of the melody, and he was ready to play. Plus, the only way to build up his immunity was to see the girl, talk to her. Get his body used to her presence, rather than fantasizing every waking second about what she was doing behind that closed door.

"And why not?" she asked, her voice drifting in. "I dare you to come out here and tell me."

"Because," he said, standing up to a million pinpricks in his calves and feet. How long had he been in that position, picking at his guitar? Could've been minutes, or hours, or days. Time seemed to stop when he was in the zone.

"Waiting," she huffed.

Never one to back down from a challenge, he walked to his door. "I'm the guy *making* the blasted music, honey. And my guitar doesn't have a knob for the volume."

"I'm sure I could help you out," she said, but she didn't sound the least bit helpful. He smirked, imagining her face twisting in a sour expression.

And just like move-in day, he was completely unprepared for what happened next. He opened the door and he couldn't breathe. He was disoriented, hit with the strangest sort of pain. It was like that time as a kid, when he popped a wheelie on his bike and fell off the back, knocking the wind clear out of his chest.

That's exactly what she did to him.

And if that first day was a teaser, with stolen looks and quick glances, this morning was the full-length feature film. And holy fuck did he get his fill. He perused her body as if he was buying a new instrument—slow and thorough, with great care.

Dressed in a tank top and those tiny little shorts women liked to wear to bed, she stood at his doorway, hands on her hips. Freaking glorious trim hips with the perfect amount of curve. And speaking of curve, the material of her top was just the right amount of tight and thin, offering him a preview of her perky breasts. He quickly snapped his mouth shut after he realized he was almost at the point of drooling. Her partially covered body was nearly the perfect combination of naughty and nice, in his humble opinion, though he could've done with just a pinch more naughty.

"Well now," he said, mustering up all of his control to keep his hands to himself. "That wasn't very neighborly."

"And banging around before the sun's up is courteous to your neighbors?" She straightened her back and pulled her lips tight, but her pink-tinged cheeks gave her away. She was affected by him as well. Maybe not to the same degree, but there was something there, he could feel it.

He gripped the doorjamb to steady himself, continuing to drink her in in small doses—even when he wanted to take a huge gulp. He shifted and said a quick prayer of thanks he wasn't wearing a loose pair of sweatpants. The denim he had on was strong enough to hold him at bay...if only for the moment.

"Just making music, sugar," he said, trying to keep his voice steady. "Trust me, you'd know if I was doing any sort of banging."

"Classy." Her cheeks were now fully flushed. When was the last time he made a woman blush? Too long, and that was a helluva shame.

"Right." He laughed. "Says the lady who prances home at five a.m., carrying her drawers in her handbag. What's the Good Book say about casting stones?"

Her mouth dropped open, and she promptly turned on a heel and walked back to her place, slamming the door once again.

"Hey," he called out, wanting to push just a little more. "I still didn't get your name."

"And you never will," she said, before the click of her deadbolt resounded in the hallway between them.

He chuckled and shook his head. Yeah, sometimes he could be a real asshole.

Chapter Three

That was twice now! Twice he had her retreating to safety. How the hell was she supposed to show her boss, her ex, and everyone in her hometown that she was a force to be reckoned with if she couldn't even handle a simple man with a guitar?

She was shaking as she made her way back inside her apartment. He surprised her. Well, the way he *looked* surprised her, though this was one surprise she didn't mind. When he opened the door, she was dumbstruck—at a complete loss for words, and that did not happen to Melody Sharp. But she had to admit she'd never been so taken by a man. He had that rugged sort of handsome cowboy appeal that was only enhanced by the fact that he desperately needed a shave and a haircut. And when his soulful brown eyes raked over her—*did* they rake over her? She wasn't sure. All she knew was that she felt it…everywhere. He wore his mass of dark hair pulled back and her hands burned to dive in and play. Then there was his mouth—full lips partially concealed by his scruff, which made everything he said seem extra dirty.

It was a good thing she didn't catch a glimpse of him the other day, because she might've made use of that mattress he was moving into his apartment on the spot. Sweet baby Jesus, she'd like to know his Sleep Number.

Mel stood there on the other side of the door, waiting for him to say something else. It was juvenile, but yelling at that big hunk-o-man was almost as enjoyable as ogling him. He really was the perfect punching bag for her frustrations. Though now he was sure to be the cause of a few new ones.

But honestly, how could someone be so rude? Playing guitar and moving flippin' furniture, at all hours? Some wannabe country music star, she bet. Sure, that music he was playing did sound really, really good—unique in a way that was more bluesy than the country pop overplayed on the radio—and, well, she'd already covered his looks. A tiny shiver traveled up the back of her neck. Oh what she could do with all that raw material!

Geez, now she was getting just plain desperate.

Of course, Mel hadn't been sleeping when she first heard the soothing strumming of the guitar. She'd been thinking of ways to handle her own troubles. She was in such a financial crisis that she was considering picking up a second job but wasn't sure she could juggle something else with Miranda on her ass.

It was her own fault. Mel had a habit of sabotaging her professional life. Her first offense was being too accommodating with her clients, who often mistook her professional attention for something personal. She lost three clients shortly after she shut down their…advances. After that, she wasn't accommodating enough, fearful that showing her clients (ninety-nine percent of them men) any extra dedication would give them the wrong idea, and that caused even more complaints. That's how these good ol' boys were. Entitled, demanding, and impossible to please. Surprisingly, Miranda stood behind her in those instances. Her boss wasn't particularly happy about it, but she had her back. What pushed the Ice Queen over the edge were Mel's late arrivals, early departures, and overall disinterest in her job. Ever since Viv moved, it had only gotten worse.

Viv Brennan was a PR star, poised for executive management. She was also Mel's best friend. She still worked for the company, remotely from her fiancé's hometown, managing Elite's new contract with NASCAR—which was how Viv met the love of her life. Jarod Cage had quickly become the darling of the racing circuit, thanks in part to Viv's big brain. Now the two were living their happy ever after. Mel was thrilled for her friend. Really. But that didn't stop her from missing her in the office every day.

It was Viv who made her realize that her clock was seriously ticking. At twenty-five, most of her friends were moving up and out in the world. That's what it felt like anyway. Neck-deep in their careers, or getting engaged, buying homes, taking amazing vacations. Or simply running wild. Yet, here she was. Stuck. And she was tired of it.

Luckily, she was going to pay Viv and Jarod a visit soon, so maybe that would set her straight. At least she'd stand a better chance of getting some sleep.

It would also help her avoid the man who had called her five times yesterday. She knew why he was calling and what he wanted. Trouble was, she didn't have it. So she'd ignore him...until she could find a way to work something out.

A few hours after her tussle with the cowboy, Mel sat absolutely captivated, listening to a modern-day feminist hero. She wasn't much for motivational speakers, or corporate functions for that matter, but Frankie Fink was one talking head she could get behind. Frankie was a marketing marvel and best-selling author of *It's Your Turn*. She traveled all over the country to help women succeed in the working world, be it as a barista at Starbucks or an executive at Sysco. The woman was brash, loud, pushy, and cursed like a sailor. Mel felt an instant camaraderie with her.

"So if you want to be heard, ladies," Frankie Fink said to the crowded auditorium. "You must push past the dicks, and take a seat at the goddamn table."

The attendees had mixed reactions to that comment—from jubilation to disgust. The hotel conference room was packed with women of all ages—power suits circa 1990 through 2015—including some of Atlanta's most influential women. One gal wearing an ill-fitting navy ensemble practically choked on her cucumber sandwich at the mention of male genitalia.

Mel giggled as she took notes about demanding respect and taking control in today's workplace.

"Don't opt out, ladies," Frankie continued. "Don't be pushed to the side. You are valuable, but you must contribute."

Too bad Mel had grown up believing her only value was to look good next to the man in her life. Support *him*.

Believe in *him*. She wasn't sure how to demonstrate her own worth. This was where Viv always brought out the best in her. Viv made it a point to publically praise Mel's efforts. She also brought her into key meetings and forced her to speak up when it mattered. Now that she was gone, Mel had no reason, or motivation, to sing her own praises or to go the extra mile at work. It never seemed to get her anywhere, anyway. What was the point?

She had the feeling Frankie would know the answer to that loaded question. The woman was a ball of energy, bouncing from one side of the stage to the other—her long red ponytail chasing behind her. She was the tall drink of water these ladies were thirsty for, Mel included. Simply listening to the presentation gave her that tingling, happy feeling that something good was about to happen. A sensation she hadn't experienced in a long time. What was it called? Hope?

Yeah, it was corny as hell. Still, it was hard *not* to get wrapped up in the moment.

Frankie pulled up the next section of her presentation, titled *Rules to Help You Rule*. She pointed her laser pen and clicked the elaborate slide show to reveal: *Rule #1—Work hard. If you can't be the smartest in the room, become the most informed.*

Mel went back to her notes. This was good stuff. She used to have the inside track on all of Elite's clients. Not because she was stalking them or trying to impress anyone, but because she was genuinely interested in people, and the tips and tidbits of information she gathered always proved important at some point in the campaign. It was then that it started to dawn on her. There was a time when she was good at her job. When she cared.

Frankie flipped the next slide: *Rule #2 — Know what you want and go for it.*

Now, that had been precisely the problem for Mel, especially lately. She didn't *know* what she wanted. Since moving to Atlanta, her existence had been strictly focused on making a life that would impress her friends and family in Sweetwater. It wasn't necessarily what she wanted; it was more about appearances.

The first year she came back for the *Last Hurrah*, she'd been working with the Falcons and was able to talk two of the big players into doing community work in her hometown. She even got them to ride on one of the floats in the parade. The second year, she brought Kevin to play the role of her new boyfriend. He played it up in a completely over-the-top way. Then over the New Year, she had Viv and Jarod join her for the party in the town square. Needless to say, they attracted attention. Now, the year Teddy was ready to come home — the year it really mattered — she had nothing.

Before she read that stupid email, she had planned on coming to the celebration without any bells and whistles. This was the year she planned on coming by herself, as herself. No more smoke and mirrors. No more distractions. Because, shoot, it was exhausting living a lie, and she didn't want to do it anymore. But how could she face them without any sort of diversion? How could she face Teddy?

Mel slammed down the rest of her coffee as the room anxiously awaited the next kernel of the guru's genius. Frankie didn't delay. She whipped through the slides.

Rule #3 — Connect and be connected. You don't have to go at it alone.

Click.

Rule #4—Play in the boys' sandbox.

Click.

Rule #5—Leave to get ahead.

It was the last one that really stuck with Mel. Frankie said women sometimes become pigeonholed in their roles, and even after they gain experience and grow, the people in charge only see a woman for what she was—not who she had become.

Maybe that's what was happening at Elite…and the rest of her life. Maybe it was time to move on. With the new Teddy development, it did seem like the Universe was giving her a sign. She could be like Scarlett—back from the trenches to return to her home a stronger woman. But to do that, she'd have to up her game at work. She wasn't going to return to Sweetwater without a solid recommendation from the Ice Queen. With that in her back pocket, she'd have her pick of jobs. She just needed to find a way to fix things with her boss.

"So"—Frankie's voice brought Mel back to the task at hand—"what tools do you need to thrive in the workplace? What are you missing?"

"The only tool I'm missing at my office is a cock," the young woman in the hideous navy suit said under her breath. She didn't look up for approval or wait for reaction like most people did when trying to be clever. She kept writing in her notebook, twirling her hair, almost oblivious to her surroundings. Was it possible there was someone in the group who hadn't fallen under Frankie's spell?

It took a second before Melody burst out laughing.

The woman's eyes darted over to her, like she'd just awoke from a dream. She'd coiled her hair so tightly, Mel thought she might pull it straight out of her head—which would be a shame because despite the mousy librarian look she had going on, the woman's auburn locks, creamy skin, and delicate bone structure were *the* definition of beauty. "Oh God. I didn't mean to say that out loud."

"Not offending anyone over here, darlin'," Mel whispered with a smile. The comic relief was more than welcome.

Mel considered the question herself. What was *she* missing to thrive? Money, ambition, drive, and intellect to name a few. At this point, the question should have been: what *wasn't* she missing? That was *her* perception anyway.

"Next I'll share some of the most effective tools to help you reach your goals," Frankie informed the audience, before dismissing them for a fifteen minute break.

Solid marketing technique, Mel noted. End on a hook so the audience has to come back for more. Nicely done, Ms. Fink. She set her notes aside and followed the woman in navy to the lobby, planning to take full advantage of the coffee and cookies laid out. On her new budget, she was forced to drink instant, and there were no treats to be had. She'd only last another month before her bank account was completely depleted.

"Hi. I'm Melody Sharp," she told the auburn haired woman when they reached the table overflowing with chocolate chip, macadamia, and oatmeal goodness. Her mouth watered. "I work at Elite PR."

"Gennifer Foley, Access Advertising." The woman extended a hand, but quickly snatched it back as she noted Melody's were already overflowing with the treats and coffee.

"So what are you in for?" Mel sipped from her cup before releasing an orgasmic groan. It was absolutely heavenly.

"What do you mean?" Gennifer nibbled on a cookie and pretended not to notice as Mel not-so-discreetly lined her purse with the baked goods.

"Does Access require you to be a member of Atlanta's Women in Business, or are you here of your own accord?" Satisfied with her haul, Mel led them away from the table to a seating area by the window that overlooked the Flatiron Building. It was her favorite in the entire city.

"I volunteered, if you can believe it." Gennifer crossed her legs, shifting uncomfortably in the horrendous calf-length skirt.

"Really?" Mel let the word hang in the air, not quite believing her answer. Of course, she would've happily come to hear Frankie speak, but the rest of the events had been a series of outdated snooze fests. She couldn't understand why anyone—especially of her generation—would attend willingly.

"Trying to learn survival skills," Gennifer explained. "I basically work for a Neanderthal who thinks I'm there to fetch coffee and look cute for the male clients."

"Well, that smells worse than bullshit." Mel glanced at her ringing phone, silencing it when she saw the name *Kevin* come up. They hadn't talked since her walk of shame, and she still wasn't ready to deal, so she ignored it. It was becoming a very bad habit. Frankie would not approve.

"Tell me about it." Gennifer smoothed her hands over her blazer. "That's why I've opted for these hideous things. Absolutely dreadful, right? I've found the uglier the clothes, the stronger the armor."

Mel did a double take and Gennifer grinned. "Oh, thank God," Mel squealed. "I didn't understand what was going on here." She waved a hand over the navy ensemble.

"Isn't it great?" she said proudly. "I have this same getup in five colors. One for each day of the week."

"Does it work?" Mel asked, wondering if maybe she should've deployed that strategy with her own more handsy clientele.

"Depends on the client," Gennifer said. "There are some hard up men in this city who even an ugly suit can't keep at bay. That's why I jumped at the chance to join the group. What about you?"

"I'm here courtesy of the Ice Queen."

"Ah, yes." Gennifer nodded. "I've heard of Miranda Wells. So *she* made you join?"

"Yes…after she demoted me." Melody grimaced, doing a quick scan around the lobby to be sure nobody else heard her. "Can't believe I said that out loud. This is usually the one day a week I can pretend that I'm not such a failure."

"What happened?" Gennifer leaned in and put her hand on Mel's arm. It was a simple gesture that almost brought her to tears. Viv had really been the only person that Mel could let her guard down with. She didn't realize how much she needed that.

So in their remaining seven minutes, Mel gave her new friend the abbreviated version of her demise at Elite.

"I don't mean to be a weirdo or anything," Gennifer said as she pulled Mel aside after the conference let out. "But would you want to go out for happy hour?"

Hmm, go for a drink with cool chick or go home and try

to hide from the guy across the hall while feasting on the crumbled cookies from her purse?

"Love to." It was no contest, and Mel had a tiny bit of room on her credit card for a small bar tab. Not really, but she'd make do.

"Okay, hang on," Gennifer said, dashing toward the bathroom. "I need to *freshen up* a bit before I'm seen in public."

"You've been in public all day."

"Oh, *this* doesn't count, silly," she took off her blazer, revealing a tight little body Jillian Michaels would envy. "Be right back."

Mel took a seat in the hotel lobby and checked her email. She had a few ideas on one of the campaigns she was working on and thought she'd run them past Miranda. She was feeling unusually optimistic about her job. Maybe she really could turn this thing around and begin to demand the respect she knew, deep down, she deserved.

Oh, that Frankie Fink was good.

Mel was feeling so upbeat, she was ready to tackle the sure-to-be-awkward call with Kevin. He picked up on the second ring, completely out of breath.

"Mel," he said, huffing away. "Hang on, I was running."

"I can call you back." Suddenly, she was second-guessing Frankie's take-the-world-by-the-balls strategy. Avoidance had always worked in the past, why change now?

"No," he barked.

"Okay, then," she said, unsure how to launch into the conversation.

"Sorry, I just really want to talk to you. Hang on."

There was some rattling on his end, and Mel practiced

what she wanted to say in her head. She'd tell him it was fun, not that she remembered much from the night. But he didn't need to know that. Then she'd go on to say she never wanted it to happen again. She realized she was definitely not in the market for a friends-with-benefits situation. From here on out, she'd take care of her needs like most available women her age—a hookup with a safe stranger or her battery-operated friend.

"Mel." He was back, this time without all the heavy breathing. "About the other night."

"It was fun." Mel sat up in her seat and cleared her throat, ready to launch into her speech.

"Fun?" He released a dull laugh that weakened her resolve. She knew she was out of practice, but dang. It couldn't've been that bad, could it? "Sweetie, you were comatose."

"I know I passed out after and I'm sorry—"

"After what?" he interrupted, his voice growing more concerned. "Wait, you don't think we *did* anything that night, do you?"

"Didn't we?" Mel whispered, as if Atlanta's finest could hear her as they chatted in small groups and traded business cards on their way out of the seminar. This conversation was beginning to sound a little like a *Who's on first?* joke, and Mel suddenly wasn't sure she wanted to know the punchline.

"God no, Mel," Kevin said in that warm way of his before she could stop him. "Nothing happened."

"Nothing?"

"Nothing." He answered what she thought was a silent question in her head. Damn him. She was hanging her hat on the fact she finally did something naughty, only to discover she…hey, wait a minute.

"Nice try," she accused. "But I woke up in your bed *naked*." Crap, turned out some ladies could hear the one-sided conversation. An older woman with a short cap of white hair and red lipstick glanced over, shaking her head.

"Don't remind me. It was quite a show," Kevin said between fits of laughter. "Incredibly determined, I'll give you that. Or you were, until you passed out."

Mel hung up and buried her head in her hands. The hits just kept on coming. Scarlett would *so* not be impressed.

"So you didn't *do it* with Kevin?" Genn asked from her perch on a bar stool at the corner high-top table. They were three shots into a discussion about her sex life, so yeah, nicknames had already been established.

"Nope," Mel said, distracted by the bartender pouring martinis from a stainless-steel shaker behind the long mahogany bar while two women at the table to her right were doing everything shy of stripping to attract his attention. So this was her competition? Hmm, it seemed to be working. The bartender flashed his dimples and flexed his biceps as he slung the drinks—which, in her opinion, was a little cheesy. But hey, this was the nature of the game. She should've been taking notes.

Genn had snagged them a prime spot for people-watching at The Red Eye—a little place one floor below street level in the Hotel District—and it was packed with herds of men in suits. Mel appreciated the diversion. Still, even as she answered Genn's question, she was unable to believe that she hadn't sealed the deal with Kevin. Upset at first, the disappointment had now faded under the dim lights of the corporate hot spot. In fact, she wasn't feeling much more than the pleasant buzz from the not-in-her-budget tequila. Thankfully, the first two rounds were picked up by some businessmen from Ohio.

"I don't get it. You're not happy with this news?" Genn licked the salt off her glass and tipped back another one. Suit Number Eight gave her an impressed nod and a high-five.

"I am." Mel toyed with her full shot glass. "He's a great guy and I don't want to mess up our friendship, especially with Viv gone. But—"

"But you wanted to be the girl who could do that. Have some fun with no strings attached?" Genn's green eyes warmed in sympathy...or understanding, Mel wasn't sure which. And actually she didn't care. She was in need of both.

"I did," she admitted. "But it's more than that. I wanted to finally *do* something. Take some kind of action for a change. Not because I should or because it's expected. I wanted to take a chance. Live a little. But when the opportunity landed in my lap, I blew it."

In between shots one and two, Mel had told her new friend all about Teddy and his email—which had led to the embarrassing situation with Kevin. But she didn't stop there. Nope, once she started talking, it all came gushing out. The non-proposal, Germany, her move to Atlanta. She hadn't told the story since she met Viv, and it irked her that it was just as painful to talk about it this time around. And, dang it, it had been years. She should *so* be over this by now! But on some gut deep level she acknowledged that it wasn't so much Teddy as everything he stood for—that perfect life she'd envisioned, which had all been one big illusion. Not to mention the fact that her daddy had been devastated by the blow. He had been more excited when Teddy gave her a promise ring after high school than he was about her college graduation. So when he dumped her in such a public way, her father took it hard. She knew he hadn't mean to hurt her, but his expectations for her had always been so low that it made it difficult to believe otherwise.

"It's not too late to do something, you know," Genn said. "When are you supposed to meet Teddy for the romantic reunion?"

"In exactly three weeks and five days." Mel cringed. Saying it aloud made it seem real. "But I don't know if I'm going to meet him."

"Doesn't matter." She pulled out her phone and opened the notes app. "You're going home for the Last Hurrah, and he's going to be there, so we use that as our deadline."

Genn Foley was pretty amazing. Not surprising. Mel had a knack for picking friends, and she knew right away that Genn was one of the good ones. And with her transformation from corporate mouse to sex kitten in the hotel bathroom in less than five minutes? Well, they were kindred spirits.

Under the ridiculous blazer she had on earlier, Genn was wearing a kelly green sleeveless blouse that set off her auburn hair and pale skin tone beautifully. She kept the same skirt, but swapped out the fashionless footwear for a pair of high wedges.

Genn pushed the lonely shot glass toward Mel, who, in turn, downed it in record time. Three shots and it was only six o'clock. Amazingly enough, she wasn't sloppy drunk. That was the trick, Genn had told her. Get your drink on early, so you can still function the next day. Plus, this was the perfect bar time to meet dependable guys—the kind with jobs and lives. Poor Genn, Mel discovered, had her share of deadbeats in her past.

"So what did you want to accomplish when you moved to the city?" her new friend asked, ready to take notes. "What were your goals?"

"Hmm." Mel thought back. It was the lowest point in her life, that was for sure. She'd felt rejected, and stupid, and mad as hell. "I wasn't so methodical about it. I didn't have a list or anything."

"That's okay," Genn said, waiting. "Let's make one now."

"Okay." Mel started ticking them off on her fingers. "I wanted a good job. I didn't want to be dependent on a man in case the rug was pulled out from me again. I wanted to go out and have fun and be wild and crazy. To try new things out of my comfort zone. And I wanted to gain experience out in the field, you know?"

Genn winked. "Oh, I know, hon."

"I guess I just wanted to become important. Someone who wasn't so easy to throw away." And there it was, the honest truth. What she'd been too proud to admit for years.

"Can I just say what an ass this Teddy was?" Genn's face twisted. She was clearly disgusted by Mel's admission. And she should be. It was pitiful, but it didn't stop it from being true.

"You sure can." Mel wiped a stray tear that managed to escape, but Genn didn't point it out. Definitely one of the good ones.

"Assss-holllllle," she sang, cupping her mouth.

"Yeah, I know." Mel did that laugh-cry thing, while Genn waved to the waitress, signaling another round.

"Don't you worry," she said, raising her glass when the drinks arrived. "I could have you married off in three weeks if you wanted. I'm great at fixing up other people. It's my own life I can't get a handle on. See anyone you like?"

Mel didn't doubt Genn's matchmaking skills. Yet when she asked the question, the only man who popped into her head was Mr. Posturepedic and his annoying guitar. He was the things fantasies were made of, but getting mixed up with her neighbor was not a smart move either.

"Hmm?" Genn teased, jiggling her shot glass with one hand and pointing with the other to a svelte guy with Clark Kent glasses and a gorgeous tailored suit. "What about him? Or him?" She redirected their focus to a muscular guy in a blue button-down.

"I'm not sure," Mel said. "But I'll know when I see him."

"Then, here's to seeing *him* tonight." She clinked her glass and another shot went down the hatch. Her belly warmed for a fourth time.

"So now that we've got the guys taken care of," Genn said. "Let's talk about work. Two brilliant women like us? Why aren't we ruling the world yet?"

"We should be ruling the world, dammit." Mel slammed her hand on the table.

Okay, so maybe the tequila is finally starting to kick in.

"Right, and to do that, we need to follow Frankie's advice—engage and become invaluable." Genn waved away another suit before he reached their table. Shit was getting serious.

"Become invaluable. I do like the sound of that." Mel imagined what it'd be like to be in Miranda's good graces for once instead of being summoned then dismissed again without so much as a look in the eye. "But how?"

"Well…" Genn tapped a finger to her lips, deep in thought. "What is one thing your boss wants more than anything?"

"New clients." Mel didn't even have to think about it. The Ice Queen's client list was revered by every agency in the South. It was Miranda's claim to fame.

"So bring her one," Genn said simply.

If only it were that easy.

Chapter Four

"I'm not going back to Nashville," Aaron said in response to his manager's latest attempt to push him back into the life he left behind. Rita Taylor, one of the biggest agents in Music City, had balls the size of Texas, and she wasn't afraid to use them. But she was also reasonable, and had a bit of a heart, which was more than he could say for the rest of the industry. And that was why he went back to her. Though at the moment, he was seriously regretting that decision.

Holding his guitar by the neck, he paced in front of his living room windows, praying for the conversation to end.

He'd re-hired Rita just two months ago, well after the new single was written. He'd waited as long as possible before bringing her in because he knew she'd be on him like stink on a skunk once he told her he wanted back in the game.

It was worse than he'd predicted. And not only with

Rita. Oh, she was hungry—that was for damn sure. But the labels weren't as desperate. Source Records loved his single. They even seemed impressed by a few of songs on the album, but they weren't ready to take him on without a test drive—especially when the album wasn't finished. It was his own fucking fault. He'd proven to be a liability and was now left to grovel.

"Can't you just stay here until the single drops?" Rita asked, working every angle. He'd probably be disappointed if she didn't. That's what he'd loved about her the first time around—her tenacity. And if he wanted to make a comeback, he needed her. The music industry, particularly the country music industry, could be forgiving if his situation was spun just right. That's what Rita did best. She was one of the few people from the past he kept in contact with, one of the few who would be part of his future.

Jayden Jones was the other.

"Rita, I want you to listen to me," Aaron said, slowly, to be sure she'd listen. "I'm not going back to Nashville." Not now, not ever. "That place brings out the worst in me. Why would I want to be there during the most important week of my year? I thought you were with me on this."

"But Jayden's here, the label's here, everyone is here," she argued. "You could get so much done. Release the single and write a few songs with your partner during your free time."

"Jayden's not my partner," he growled, insulted that even his manager didn't believe he could do this on his own.

"Calm down. You know what I mean."

Aaron's relationship with his former guitar player and co-writer was...complicated. And selfish. Though it was

Aaron with the ulterior motive this time. It was Aaron who'd decided to go solo, despite Jayden's interest in joining him. That didn't go over well, but Aaron held firm because he knew it was the only way he'd be able to play music again. He needed complete control. Yet so far he'd only managed to get through a few songs without Jay's help.

He had always believed that it was the partying and the lifestyle that had got him into his ruts the first time around. But here he was—older, experienced, and stone-cold sober—and he hadn't been able to write himself out of a paper bag. Sure he wrote the single, and it was great. But it had taken him almost a year to finish it. The other two songs took almost as long. So if he wanted to finish his comeback album in this century, he'd have to bring in Jayden. Hell if that didn't sting. The guy had always been his crutch. His biggest ally and worst influence.

His best friend.

"I'm calm, I'm calm," he told Rita. "But did you ever think I might not need Jay for this?"

"Are you writing again?"

"Yes, as a matter of fact, I am." He wouldn't tell her that his new, untouchable neighbor had become his muse. Or that the song was nowhere near done.

"How many songs have you finished? Do we have an album yet?" She fired off her questions. "Send them over so I can—"

"Hold up there," he interrupted. "I said I was writing again, not that I finished any songs yet."

There was a long sigh on the other side and then a long pause. "How about if Jayden comes down to see you?"

His head ached at the thought. They'd been inseparable

since they were kids, but he rarely saw him these days. Back in the day, they were both in trouble constantly. Jayden simply loved living on the edge. He had a restless spirit and an addiction to the wild side…among other things.

For Aaron, it was because of a lack of any sort of parental guidance. His mom was a singer as well, on the road for most of his childhood and all of his kid brother's formative years. She only came home after his daddy lost the fight with his kidneys. He'd been sick, on dialysis, for years until one day, he just didn't wake up.

His mama was not happy to return home, especially once it was clear she could no longer go out on the road. So she dedicated her new life to the bottle. It didn't take long for the money to dry up and, well, the rest of Aaron's childhood made for helluva good lyrics.

In the end, music was the only way out for him. By the time he and Jayden were out of high school, they had a record deal. But man, it sure didn't take care of everything. Growing up without anyone looking out for him… It leaves a kid empty. And he tried to fill that space with everything imaginable. It was easy to do with all the money and fame. But as rough as it was for him, it was worse for Jayden. His family had given up on him long ago, only showing up when they wanted something.

They'd both crashed hard and damn near lost it all—the band, the label, most of the money. Shoot, they were lucky to make it out alive. But for Aaron, he had something to snap him the hell out of it. Someone who needed him—his little brother, Graham.

Jayden wasn't as lucky.

"Just think about it," Rita encouraged.

Aaron grumbled. He wanted to play music more than anything, but he needed boundaries. He wasn't strong enough otherwise, he knew that. With his mama's genetics and his own track record, he needed stability. And hell, he was on shaky ground. Source Records was the only label willing to give him any kind of a shot.

The only way he'd make it was by following the rules he made up before jotting down the first note on the single: no Nashville, no band, no distractions. Because if this didn't work, it was back to small time gigs and a struggle for both him and his brother.

"Look, I'm trying to save your career," Rita said, while Aaron stared out the window, only half listening now. "Isn't that what we agreed on? One more shot. Well, this is it, baby, and if you don't grab it now, I'm not sure there's going to be another."

"I'm grabbing my shot, don't you worry," he said, right before a raucous screaming started outside his apartment. "But I'm going to do it my way."

"I know, I know," Rita conceded, as Aaron moved to the window to see what was going on out front. "Okay, Atlanta isn't that far. Others have managed to do it living in different locales, but you'll have to be flexible. For once in your life."

Aaron tried to ignore the ruckus outside and focus on Rita. This was important stuff. But he wasn't able to turn away. He watched an extremely pissed off woman mix it up with a taxi driver out on the street. Man, she was ticked all right. Her hand gestures told him that much. The black high heel kicking the cabbie's door told him something else. Shit, of all the places to move, he had to end up sharing a building with a party girl. That was all he needed.

Just walk away, Major. Do not *get involved.*

"Aaron? Hello?" Rita's voice pulled him to the task at hand.

"You act like I can't be accommodating," he said, stretching his neck. It'd been a long two days, and he was tired and achy. That's all this was. Exhaustion. They'd need to table this discussion until he could concentrate for more than two minutes at a time. "Listen, I need to go. I have a bunch of unpacking to do. Let me get settled and we'll finish this discussion later."

"Fine. But just a friendly reminder, if you don't have your launch party in Nashville, the label won't pay for it. So you're going to have to figure that out. And you need an event to kick this thing off, Aaron. I'm not going to budge on that point."

He cringed, thinking about the dwindling status of his bank account.

"Mmm-hmm." He pulled the phone away from his ear.

"Also, don't forget about the image consultant," she yelled as if she could see what he was doing. "I'm done with that lumbersexual thing you have going!"

Aaron didn't have the foggiest idea what she was talking about. He made it his business not to know. He also didn't understand the need for all the bells and whistles. Why couldn't he just make music for the people without having it turn into such a goddamn production? There had to be a better way.

But at that moment, all he could think about was the show going on in the front lawn, and whether his new neighbor was okay out there. He took another look…just to see if she needed help.

It didn't seem like it. She was livid, still yelling at the cab driver. Man alive, did she come in any other flavor?

Aaron wasn't sure if he said good-bye to Rita, because the angry gal on the street demanded his full attention. She was spectacular with all those blond curls bouncing around her flushed face. She scowled and quite possibly cursed. He wasn't sure; he couldn't make out the words.

Her silky top was in the same state as her hair—disheveled and misbehaving. It was untucked from a pair of sleek black pants. They hugged her gentle curves, and hell, it made his mouth water. Then she said something else to the taxi driver and flipped him off. That had Aaron busting a gut. If anything, she was good entertainment.

He resigned himself to going outside and getting a front-row view of the show in one of those comfortable chairs on the front porch. And help her out, if she needed it.

Turned out he didn't have to, because seconds later the show came to him.

She was mumbling as she made her way up the stairs. He moved to the door to listen and was rewarded with the click of her heels on the wooden steps…a curse word in between each stride. If their first two meetings didn't do it, this sure as hell did. He was absolutely enthralled by the foul-mouth belle.

"Take a seat at the table, my ass," she muttered. "Who the hell does that woman think she is? Oh shit, there are so many stairs."

He had his eye to the peephole, waiting to see her. It was torture, but he didn't want to reveal himself. Not yet. Then it was still. No clicking. No swearing.

Aaron couldn't help himself. He had to know what was

going out there. And more than that, he had to officially meet this woman who could put his dirty mouth to shame. He. Wanted. Her. Name.

Just as he was about to open the door, he caught a glimpse of her. She messed with her door for a moment and then launched into a full-blown hissy fit.

"That cheap bastard!" she screamed. Aaron looked on as she pounded on the door to her apartment. But it was no use. It was paddle-locked shut, a shiny lockbox hanging from the doorknob.

Oh, hell no. She was a rent dodger? Strange, she didn't seem the type. Though why else would her apartment be locked up without her apparent knowledge? And when had that happened, anyway? He hadn't heard a peep across the hall since their morning run-in. Then again, he had been writing all day.

He cracked the door open to find that she'd dropped to the ground. And she was crying—the one thing he couldn't handle.

"What am I going to do now?" Her body shook in a sad little puddle. His insides twisted, remembering that feeling of helplessness. He'd been there.

Aaron gritted his teeth and opened the door. He had no choice. He couldn't just leave her out there. He would, however, keep his hands off her. No matter how difficult it may be. The last thing she needed to deal with now was his depraved fantasies.

"I can't do anything right," she cried.

"Hey," he said, walking out into the hall. "What's going on? It can't be all the bad, can it?"

"It is," she said, wiping her nose on her arm, just like he

did in elementary school. "It so is. You can go ahead, make your fun."

"Hey now, I don't kick people when they're down. Why don't you come into my place, and we'll figure this out." He extended a hand and pulled her upright. Evidently a little too hard, because she fell into his chest, her lush lips grazing the side of his neck as he caught her. He went instantly hard, feeling an immediate and desperate urge to get her inside and show her *his* kind of fun. Instead, he set her on her feet and opened the door. "Go on in."

Aaron told her to have a seat and then went to the kitchen to buy himself some time. For two days he had allowed this girl to consume his every waking thought—she had him so jacked up it was physically painful. Now she was in his apartment with no place to go. The big guy upstairs must really hate his guts.

"What are you doing in there?" she called out.

Good question.

He looked around the room, his eyes landing on the coffee pot. "Making coffee," he said. "You look like you could use some."

"I'm not drunk," she slurred, just a bit.

"Mmm-hmm." He went about making a full pot, extra strong. "Well, don't take this the wrong way, but you smell like a frat party on Cinco de Mayo."

"That's because someone spilled a drink on me," she spat.

And there was the firecracker. That was better—he could deal with her.

"What about the tears and all the babbling?" he asked, rounding the corner with two hot mugs. She was curled up on his couch, the top buttons on her blouse undone, and showing more tanned skin than should be legal. They must've popped open when she took to kicking the taxi. He tightened his grip on the cup handles, working to keep from spilling scalding coffee on his hands.

"I've been kicked out of my apartment and am royally screwed, I think I'm entitled to a little pity party." She took the cup he offered and wrapped her hands around the cup. "Thank you…"

"Aaron." He filled in the blank for her. "Aaron Major." He raised a brow as he looked down at her.

"Melody Sharp." She answered his silent question with the tiniest of smiles. "It's nice to finally have a name for the man who's been keeping me up for the past two days."

Tell me about it.

"Do I need to remind you that one of those nights was all you, honey?" He took a seat in the leather chair across from her, willing himself not to think about the panties that fell from her purse during their first meeting.

"Right." She nodded. "But you didn't help matters that morning."

"And I am sorry about that," he lied, trying to focus on his distraught neighbor's problems instead of her impossibly plump lips. Christ, he shifted in his seat before his thoughts became obvious to Melody as well.

"It doesn't matter now." She sniffled in between sips of her coffee.

"What do you mean?" he asked, not following her train of thought in the least.

"We're no longer neighbors." Her eyes were wide, glossed over slightly, and damn if she didn't tug on his heartstrings… and other areas as well. Areas he'd agreed to ignore when he opened his door to her. "So you can play your music or move your furniture whenever you want."

"But what if I'd rather scrap with you?" He was surprised just how much he enjoyed that little adrenalin rush the past few mornings. Truth was, he'd already been looking forward to their next run-in. "So tell me what happened and maybe we can fix it."

Melody stared at him for the longest time before her guarded gaze seemed to warm. "I was late on rent again," she finally admitted. "I guess Cole decided enough was enough. Thing is, I would've had it to him in a few weeks, but I guess it's too late."

"Are you sure you don't want to talk to him?" he pushed. "Try to work something out?" He couldn't understand it for the life of him, but he didn't want to see her leave.

She shook her head.

"What about the guy?" He felt irritation in his throat, but surely the guy keeping her up until all hours of the night would help. Then again, the asshole hadn't even seen her inside safely. Still, he had to ask. "The panties-in-the-purse guy? I can give you a ride to his place if you want."

"No, my situation is hopeless," she said, not giving anything else away. She just chewed on her lip, making it increasingly difficult for him to concentrate. "But there *is* something you could do to help."

"Anything," he blurted before he even heard what she had to say.

"Really?" she asked, hopeful, and heck if he wasn't thrilled to put that look there. But then why did he have the sinking feeling that he just bought himself a world of trouble?

The hell-on-heels spitfire he'd grown so fond of in the past few days had dissolved into a sad and lonely character that could've been in one of his songs. Her mischievous eyes were now red and puffy and there was no more swivel in that glorious step. She was careful and timid as she walked into the room, and that made him feel things he didn't want to name.

Of course, the old Aaron would've had that naughty belle on top of him riding reverse cowgirl before they even exchanged names—whether she was devastated or not—because he knew it would do them both a world of good. But he was no longer that guy. Didn't want to be. Though somebody needed to inform his dick, which liked the old Aaron, thank you very much, and was saddled up and ready to go.

Even though Melody was a few drinks past tipsy, she didn't look at all comfortable when she asked if she could crash at his place until morning. With tear-stained cheeks and a broken voice, she spoke so quiet he had a hard time hearing her. When he did, it about killed him. He had the feeling she'd never asked anyone for a favor before.

It was Melody's lucky day because the new Aaron was all about second chances and he wasted no time agreeing to let her stay in the guest room. Alone. He also spent the better part of an hour listening to her story. She told him about her ex, who never really treated her like anything more than arm candy, his own personal trophy. Hell, Aaron hated hearing about him so much, he was tempted to go to Sweetwater and give him a homecoming he'd never forget. Then there was her boss, who sounded like a real ball-buster, and her best friend who'd moved hours away. He retained it all, even as his eyes took in each and every tempting inch of her body.

"What about you, Aaron Major?" she asked, testing the bed in the spare room. He hated where his mind went at seeing her there. On a bed. At his place. More than that, he hated the people who extinguished her fire and left her in such a state. He much preferred the girl outside, kicking in cab doors. "Ever have such an epically shitty day? Or year? Or three years?" She laughed, but it was hollow…fake, and it make his gut ache.

Hell yes, he'd been there before. The fact that it was his own doing, or mostly his own doing, didn't lessen the painful memory. He wouldn't wish it on anyone. So if he could help her find a way out of this shitty-ass situation, even if only for a night, he was determined to do just that.

"You'd be surprised." He bent over and helped her with her shoes before folding back the covers for her. The room was set up for Graham, who wouldn't be staying with him until the holidays, but Aaron never felt settled until he had a place ready for his teenage brother. He wondered if he would've been so inclined to offer Melody a place to stay if he didn't have the extra space. Saving damsels in distress wasn't exactly his typical M.O.

"Surprised by what?" she prodded, when he didn't finish answering her question.

"I've actually had several shitty years, if you must know." He grabbed a pillow and began smacking it in an effort to fluff it for her. Why? He didn't have a goddamn clue. It was something he remembered his dad doing before he tucked him in at night. But from the look on her face, he was using more force than he needed to.

"What'd that pillow ever do to you?" She pulled it out of his hands.

"Just trying to make you comfortable, I guess." He leaned against the wall, suddenly itchy without something to do. His instincts had him aching to take care of what ailed her, the good ol' fashioned way. Still, there was a stronger need to see her safe. To protect her. He was tucking her into bed for Christ sakes. In the spare room!

"I really appreciate all this, you know," she said, settling into the bed. "And if I was around when you were having your shitty years, I would've done the same."

No, you wouldn't have, honey.

He hated to even think about the people who stuck around for him during those dark days. He would never put anyone through that again, which was why he vowed to avoid distractions, namely relationships. Poor Graham was stuck with him, but he could avoid bringing anyone else into the freak show that was the music business.

"Here." He threw Mel a T-shirt to change into. "You can sleep in this." Then he left the room to retrieve aspirin and a tall glass of water…and to calm his frayed nerves. He hadn't been around a woman like Mel in a long time, and she made him jittery.

When he returned, jitters were the least of his worries. Tucked into the bed, looking small and lost amid the pillows and blankets, with her hair fanned out around her face, Mel turned her lips in a sad smile that nearly did him in. It was even worse than the tears she shed earlier. He had the nagging urge to slide in next to her and hold her until she fell asleep, which was completely out of the question, so he sat beside her on the edge of the bed and extended the glass instead.

She took it, draining every drop, though she insisted she was no longer drunk.

"I feel like hell," she said then, turning on her side and reaching out for his hand.

Her sweet gesture hit him in all the wrong places—primarily his heart. Yet when he took her offering, the contact sent his mind back into the gutter. Her hand was soft and small in his grip, her skin so friggin' hot to the touch. "What do you want me to do?" He stroked her cheek with his other hand, unwilling to let go.

What the hell was happening here?

"Make me feel better?" she beseeched him.

That was easier said than done. He doubted she had any idea how deeply her innocent request affected him. No sir. 'Cause if he'd learned anything from the blubbering coffee cup confessional out on the living room sofa, it was that Miss Melody Sharp had never quite recovered from the way her ex had treated her. And she definitely didn't see herself clearly, or understand just how fucking appealing she was. That asshole put that doubt there.

"Darlin', I'm no good at offering advice or saying the right thing. Really, there are only two things I can do to make a woman feel better."

"Two is better than most. Pick one?" Her blue eyes pleaded, and he had the strangest desire to please her.

Of course, his go-to in times like these involved getting horizontal—or vertical, he wasn't picky. His dick pulsed behind his zipper, clearly voting for option number one, which was exactly why his brain opted for go-to number two.

He went into the other room and brought back his guitar, always his fall back. He could do this for her, no problem, get lost in the music for a spell, and maybe she'd drift off to sleep.

He went back to his post at the edge of the bed and began playing his new song for her—the album single. Her eyes went wide when he sang the first note, low and soft. The song was about new beginnings and second-chances and shit the country music industry had lived on forever. But it was also about crossroads. It was about where he was in his life—where, he realized, Mel was too. Sure, she might have defeat in her eyes, but there was still a fire. She wasn't going down without a fight. He admired that. Even more, he admired how she looked in his T-shirt. He swallowed, realizing he could just make out the tips of her nipples under the cotton, and he cursed himself for it. All the while, he kept playing.

She closed her eyes as the rhythm of the strings filled the room. He plucked them for her, turning his head to his guitar as he went into another song. By the time he hit the third one, he was sure she'd fallen asleep.

He rose slowly, not wanting to jostle her, and crossed the smooth wood floor. As he reached for the door, she said, "Now what about that second thing you do…"

Chapter Five

Aaron stopped dead in his tracks, taking a sharp inhale, before turning around. That was good. It meant he wasn't beyond convincing.

Mel lifted to her elbows—a move that made the huge V-neck T-shirt that Aaron gave her slip off her shoulder. Well, she was good and screwed now, so what the hell? She decided to go for it. Because she suspected that *other thing* he could do to make a woman feel good had nothing to do with his guitar. He so willingly gave her the first, but could she convince him to give her the second? Judging by his expression as moved to face her, it wouldn't be a difficult task. She ached to know just how skilled those fingers of his were.

Her first shot at a hookup may have been a bust, but for reasons she couldn't explain, she wanted to try again. Not just because she was down and out, or because she hadn't been touched in a millennium. It was this particular man she wanted, as crazy at that sounded.

He'd been so patient with her as she told him her sob story, why she'd come to Atlanta. The tequila buzz helped make her comfortable enough to share, but he was also a really good listener. And now that she had pretty much everything taken from her, she also had no fear left to hold her back.

Things had been financially tight since her boss put her on probation, and the pay cut made rent all but impossible. Still, Mel never thought her landlord would completely cut her off. Of course, all she had to do to get rid of her money problems was to call her daddy. But that would mean she'd lived up to those low expectations he had of her. He never thought she was cut out to be a *working gal*. No, that role was for her sister—the smart one. Mel was his pretty girl, and he wanted her at home in Sweetwater where he could marry her off to a suitable man who would take care of her. Heck, he really wanted her at home, ready and waiting, when Teddy decided to make his way back.

Looked like he was going to get his wish.

So Mel had to make the most of every second she had left. She was going back home, plain and simple, but she was going out with a bang. And she meant that quite literally. From the second she heard Aaron's voice, something sparked inside her. And once she got a good look at him, her body came alive. Forget Scarlett, it was Mel who "should be kissed, and often, by someone who knew how." She was certain Aaron Major knew how.

It was in his smoky eyes, the timbre of his voice, the cool, assured way he carried himself. This cowboy knew his way around music, and with a body like his, she was confident he knew his way around a woman, too. He was just so...so sexy.

Especially standing there in the dark, torn about what to do. At least, she hoped he was torn.

"Baby, you don't want to know about that," he purred, which only made her want to know more. Though, despite her limited experience, she had a pretty good idea.

"I think I do." She let the sheet drop in a very Scarlett-like move. The V-neck of his T-shirt draped lower. His reaction was audible, and the sound shot right between her legs.

"I don't think that's a smart idea," he said, shaking his head. "Aren't you involved with someone? I understand if you don't want to crash there or call him this late, but damn, I'm really trying to do the right thing here." He set his guitar up against the wall and took a step forward, deliberately locking his eyes on hers. Still, she saw them dip a few times.

"I'm not involved with anyone," she told him. "And what you thought you saw that morning we first met? Not what you think. Nothing happened. Turns out I can't even have a one-night stand without screwing it up." Suddenly, she wanted this so badly that she was having a hard time staying under those covers at all. She squeezed her thighs together in an effort to soothe the ache between them. He ignited something in her that demanded his attention, and she was willing to beg if she had to.

"I truly doubt that, darlin'." He sat on the bed again, considering her. He smelled like cedar and vanilla, maybe from the guitar. She didn't know, didn't care. She just wanted to get closer to his scent. To that tanned, muscular column of his neck, the strong line of his jaw. He was raw and rugged perfection, and she wanted to touch him. He leaned in, his full lips opened slightly, which had her mindlessly nibbling on her own. And though his hair was still pulled back, rogue strands escaped and fell around his face. She reached up to toy with one of them, rubbing the silky wisp between her fingers.

"I'm trying to change, Melody," he said as he took her hand, tracing tiny circles on the inside of her wrist before allowing a single finger to travel up her arm. "I used to be the kind of guy who took what he wanted, when he wanted it. That guy would've had you inside his apartment and bent over his sofa that very first time he saw you, and he wouldn't have cared if you had just been with another man or not."

Those words should've been crude to her, but they weren't. They made her body tingle and her core throb with need. There was a part of her that wished he had tried something with her that first time. Or the second. Was that crazy? Absolutely. But all reason went out the window where this man was concerned.

This time, she wouldn't let the opportunity slip through her grasp. She owed herself that much. Yes, it was risky. She didn't even know the man, or what he did for a living. But wasn't that the excitement of a one-night stand? Wasn't it time she was a little restless? Plus, she knew first-hand how strict Cole was about his tenants. There was no way Aaron would be here if he had any sort of record.

She'd taken inventory of the place: no photos of a wife, a girlfriend, or a kid. He didn't have a ring finger tan line, and he definitely didn't put off the creeper vibe.

Jesus, Mel. Just stop thinking for once in your life.

Not so easy to do when the cowboy stroked his finger along her scorching skin. And once that lonely finger reached the base of her neck, she couldn't take it any longer.

With a quick breath, she gripped his palm and placed it over her heart, which had a wild rhythm of its own playing in her chest.

He groaned, and it only encouraged her.

Beat.

She led his hand to where the neckline of the shirt dipped in a deep V, exposing several inches of her bare flesh. Hot damn, it was thrilling. For all her talk, she had never directed a man before. Never.

Beat. Beat.

She moved their fingers to the edge of the soft fabric… beat…before coaxing him inside the thin cotton barrier. But once their hands snaked under her shirt, he took over. She leaned into his touch, never taking her eyes off him. The shirt gaped further, allowing him free rein. Mmm, she was right about his skills.

He lay down beside her and met her anxious, lustful stare as he caressed her breasts, lavishing his undivided attention on one and then the other, teasing her aching nipples to hardened peaks. "You bring back all those feelings, Mel. You make me remember what it's like to be consumed and out of control, and I can't go back to that."

"I'll be gone by tomorrow," she reminded him. "And this will only be a memory. You don't have to worry." She wiggled closer, trying to find some friction to ease the mounting pressure at her center.

He noticed and pushed his taut thigh between her legs. The contact felt so good, her head fell back as she took in the pleasure. "I can take care of that ache, honey. I don't think I can take you in the way you want, but I can give you relief."

Reaching his other hand under the bed sheet, he groaned

again when he found her damp panties. "Let me take care of you," he said, as every fiber in her body screamed yes, yes, yes.

She reached for him, but he shifted and pinned her arms down by her sides before she made contact.

"This is all for you," he said. "Only you. And I'm going to get you off so fast and hard, you'll be thinking about it on your wedding day."

And there went the throbbing again.

She should've been appalled or disgusted…or had *some* kind of sickened reaction to his dirty talk. Who was *he* to speak to her in that way? This should feel wrong. It *was* wrong. Yet his words had quite the opposite effect, which freaked her out a little, if she was being honest. All she could think was: more please.

"But where should I start?" he asked, pulling the sheet the rest of the way off her body. "I have so much to work with here."

Aaron lifted the hem of the shirt, inching it over her sensitive skin, little by little, until the undersides of her breast were exposed. "God, I fucking love this," he said. "The slope of your breasts, so soft and creamy. Christ, you're gorgeous, Melody."

She wanted him to lift the fabric higher. She wanted the warm air to kiss her nipples. She wanted him to look at her. All of her. She pushed her chest out slightly, unable to stop herself.

He responded the way she wanted, moving the shirt.

Higher…

Higher…

Until he pulled it over her head, and she was completely

revealed to him.

"For the past two nights, this is all I've been able to think about." He tossed the shirt on the floor and moved closer to her, and when he sighed, the heat of his breath teased her tight peaks. "Ever since those little panties fell out of your purse, I've wanted to put my hands on you."

Melody arched her back as those rough hands took what they wanted. He was confident is his every move as he explored her body, and it was so off-the-charts hot, she had to turn her head away from his gaze. She was all but panting by this point and didn't want him to see, but he wouldn't have it. He tipped her face back to his, concerned with her every reaction. He studied her, gauging each response.

It made her feel so incredibly…wanted.

Sure, she'd known her effect on men. A pretty girl in pageants, at her father's side, or on Teddy's arm. But she was only a decoration. And though she was once again exposed and on display, this was different. She couldn't put it into words, though. Didn't want to. She simply was going to enjoy every morsel of pleasure this cowboy was offering.

She felt a lift on the mattress and then his breath on her chest again. Her nipples tightened even further, if that was possible.

"Christ," he mumbled before he took his first taste. He sucked her tight bud into his mouth, warm and wet and sublime. Mel saw stars, and her head started to spin. She reached out for him, wanting to hold on, but he locked her hands again. He tasted her for a second time and growled, "This isn't going to work."

She began to protest, but he simply put a finger to her lips. He leaned over the bed and reached for something on the floor. Mel prayed it was a condom. But when he pulled himself upright, it wasn't a foil packet in his hand. It was the T-shirt.

He flashed an evil little grin and went to work on her hands, somehow banding both her wrists together above her head

The control she always possessed dissolved. She was in his care, trusting him to give her what she needed. But how she wanted to touch him and do her own exploring. She wanted to strip him of his flannel, release that wild mane and let her hands feast on him.

"I'd like to touch you." Her words synced with the images in her head, though she hadn't signaled her mouth to say them. It was like a dream—she was partially there, partially on some other plane. Being tied up and in his complete control left her deliciously unstable and out of sorts.

"Let me?" she begged.

After Aaron hit it big for the first time, he had women lining up out the door to service him. They didn't know him. He didn't know them. He never saw—or really thought about—them again. And he knew that made him an asshole.

It wouldn't be that way with Melody. He wouldn't be likely to forget her anytime soon—he was sure of it. He'd give her one last memory before she moved back to her small town to get married and start popping out babies.

Oh, he could definitely do that.

What he couldn't do was let her touch *him*.

If that happened, all bets were off. He couldn't remember

the last time a woman affected him this way. Jesus, he'd been hard for two days just watching her, listening to her voice, imagining what she was doing behind her closed door. It was messing with his head, and he didn't want her squirming her way in any deeper.

He put the kibosh on her request. "I will be the only one doing the touching tonight."

Then he went on to pepper her chest with feather-light kisses. She was so fucking soft, so perfect. But it was her scent that really did him in. Spicy. Exotic. It didn't match her prim exterior. Then again, neither did her mouth. She'd win against him in a cursing contest, hands down.

Why did he like that so much? Maybe because few people surprised him anymore.

And for that reason, he would allow himself this one thing. Slowly, quietly, he descended on her mouth. So close her breath got lost in his scruff. He knew he'd be regretting that later. For now, he indulged…and nipped at her plump lip. Her mouth had taunted him since the first time he got a good look at her. He imagined she'd taste like a ripe peach. She was sweeter. He could do this, just this, all night and never tire of it.

Aaron pulled her to him and Mel opened her mouth in invitation. He accepted and delved in, stroking his tongue over hers, again and again, until he coaxed the softest moans from her lips.

Her eyes closed, and delicate hands fisted in the restraints as he continued his exploration and changed the playful kiss to something decidedly slower, deeper, before pulling away to look at her again.

But she didn't like that. "More," she cried.

Fuck.

He descended again. But this time, it was Mel who attacked. She took her own nip of his lower lip, a move that sent shock waves to his dick. He couldn't help himself as he pushed into her.

Shit, he could so easily lose himself in this wild, complicated, stubborn girl. He wanted to, but he wasn't about to go back on his word. He needed to finish this...and fast.

"You're going to like this," he said as he snuck his hands down her naughty black panties. He expected her to be wet—he knew that from his test touch—but he wasn't prepared for her to be drenched. Or burning up. Or completely bare. He palmed that hot, smooth skin and bit his tongue to stifle a moan. This was for her. He would do this to prove a point. He'd changed. This time it was going to be different.

"Aaron," she gasped. "Don't stop."

"I don't intend to," he said as he slowly pushed one finger inside.

Mel gasped, her eyes wide. Damn, she was tight. No problem, he knew how to handle that. Slowly, he worked his way in with gentle lazy strokes, but when her entire body went rigid, he stilled.

Shit, shit, shit.

"Are you okay?" He'd never forgive himself if he hurt her.

"It's okay. Don't stop."

She wasn't lying about the other night. Clearly, it'd been a long time. Why did he like that so much? Because he was one sick bastard, that's why.

Aaron took his time, enjoying each touch, each taste of her lips, her neck, her breasts. Mel began to move against his hand, so he gradually added a second finger—even slower than he did the first.

Her moans told him he was doing just fine. She was tight, but his fingers quickly began to stretch her. He couldn't stop the images of something else stretching her, filling her. Once he was sure she was ready, he thrust those two fingers deep inside. He relished her reactions too much to take it slow.

He pumped his hand vigorously. It was time to finish this, before he lost all control.

"Please untie my hands," she said. "I need to hold on."

It was a plea that took his breath away. She needed more from him than a quick rub to get her off. She needed a connection too. He understood that. No matter how he lied to himself over the years, he completely understood.

He untied the shirt and whipped it off. Her hands grabbed him, kneading his shoulder like a kitten—like she couldn't get enough. She pulled herself up, and his arm involuntarily wrapped around her to hold her to him. She buried her head in the crook of his neck.

He didn't relent. She was tightening, gripping his fingers now. So, so hot.

His dick pulsed behind his pants, wanting to make its way toward the heat.

He still didn't let up But he pulled his fingers out long enough to tease her clit before diving in again. She pushed against his hand.

"That's it, baby," he said, hoping he could quickly talk her over the edge before he came in his pants. "Ride it out. Take what you need. Damn, you are so wet, so fucking sexy. I want to bury myself so deep inside I don't come out for days."

She released a loud moan and dug her nails into his shoulder. Good, it was working. Her breath burned his neck as her breathing grew quick and shallow. It wouldn't be long now.

"Christ, woman, if anyone knew what you kept beneath those prim, girlie clothes. Nobody would expect your greedy needs. How did I get lucky enough to find out? You are a goddamn fantasy."

Mel whimpered and arched her back, her tight little body squeezing his hand. Her lips parted and he was sure he'd never seen anything so beautiful—that full mouth and flushed skin. Her breath hitched and he knew what would follow, so he increased the pressure in long, hard strokes.

"I'm going to come," she said, completely confident. Not embarrassed, not ashamed or shy about it.

Good God.

"Do it, Melody. Now, darlin'. Come right here on my hand."

And that did it.

Her eyelids fluttered and her mouth dropped open, before her head fell back, the pulse pounding in her beautifully arched neck. Aaron took a little nip, wanting to share in this as much as he could, not wanting it to end.

Her hips pumped, and his hands worked her slower now, deeper, allowing her to ride the wave. And when he felt that final contraction around his fingers, he pulled her close.

Chapter Six

So yeah, she just got played by the cowboy. Deliciously, expertly, utterly played. Her mind was swimming. Here, all this time she'd been wanting—waiting—to do something wild, uninhibited, completely out of character, and it finally happened just as she had to leave. Or should she say, was *forced* to leave.

She didn't know which her landlord deserved more: a punch to the junk for kicking her out of her apartment so suddenly, or a party in his name for creating the opportunity for her wild night.

Aaron Major had tied her up, whispered filthy things in her ear, and worked her over until her body hummed. Oh, she grew achy just thinking of it. And what was *that* all about? In her experience, once was usually enough to satisfy her appetite. Tonight? She could've gone at that man buffet-style.

"So how was that for you?" Aaron asked, pulling her to

his side so they were face to face.

"You mean my screaming and panting didn't give me away?" She felt no need for pretense. She'd basically told him her whole life story before he'd even laid a hand on her. Most guys would've cut her off, or made a move, or pretended to listen as their eyes glazed over. Even Teddy had been guilty of that on more than one occasion. But Aaron seemed truly interested. And, for once...*she* was making the moves. Still, even with her begging, he wouldn't let her reciprocate.

That was one for the record books.

"Maybe I just want to hear it from your lips," he drawled, in that lazy country way that made her want to lick every inch of him. He tucked her post-orgasmic hair behind her ear, waiting on her response. He wasn't running out the door or drifting off to sleep, and dang, that unnerved her a little.

"What I call it is a fond-ass farewell. Going out in style." She ruffled his untamed locks, which had completely come out of the tail at the back of his neck, and tried not to darken the mood. Lord knew she didn't need to get all emotional about some random hookup when she was leaving. "What about you? Are you sure I can't show you my... appreciation?"

"I'm sure." He released a shaky sigh that made her wonder if he really was. "And trust me, I enjoyed myself very much. You might be one of the most fascinating women I've ever met."

And then he had to go and say that.

She'd been pursued before, wanted, loved even, but she'd never been taken care of in this way. And she'd never been called *fascinating* in her life.

"So what are you going to do next, Melody Sharp?"

he asked, in a welcome change of topic. "What's your next chapter look like?"

"Well," she said, absently tracing a circle on his chest with her finger. She snatched it away once she realized what she was doing,

"Hey," he said, taking her hand back to its previous location. "That kind of touching is okay."

His smile put her at ease. His entire demeanor did. For someone who could whip her into a frenzy with a word or touch, he could also calm her in much the same way.

"Fine," she teased. "But can you at least lose the cowboy shirt?"

He rolled his eyes, but sat up and unbuttoned his shirt. And holy hell, when he tossed the ugly garment aside, she was not prepared for the chiseled surface that was his chest. "Better?" he asked.

Honey, you have no idea.

"Much." Her voice cracked a smidge as she patted the bed for him to resume his horizontal position, but she covered her awe by going back to drawing those misshapen circles. Warmth bloomed under her skin once again.

"As you were saying…"

"Right, the next chapter." She kept her eyes focused on her finger as it grazed the smooth, wide expanse of his chest. "Well, since I've basically hit rock bottom, I think it's time to concede to Atlanta and go back home. The city gave me a run for my money, but now I'm homeless, broke, with only half the job I started out with."

"Hold on there." He pulled her chin up, his eyes searching. "You can't let one setback stop you."

"It's more than one setback. My God, my apartment is

on lockdown. As of this moment, I have only one pair of underwear to my name."

"Okay, you might not believe this, but I've been in a very similar predicament."

"Yeah, but guys don't mind going commando," she joked, slapping his chest. Geez, it was hard as granite.

"I'm serious," he said, so passionately that the tiny hairs on the back of her neck stood on end. "You'll be able to get your stuff back from Cole. He can't legally keep it. And if the Ice Queen really wanted you out, she would've shown you the door. From what you've told me, she doesn't seem the type to second-guess herself. If she's willing to invest in you, that tells me you must have something to offer."

Mel had never thought about in that way. She couldn't see past the blow to her ego when Miranda delivered the news. But he was right. Her boss was a hard-nosed businesswoman who had no trouble getting what she wanted and no qualms about firing people, so there had to be a reason why she kept her around.

Maybe she needed to find out what it was.

"Think about it," he said, sitting up now. "You're welcome to stay here in the spare room for a night or two until you figure it out. But you'll have to find something more *substantial* to wear to bed."

"What's it matter, if I sleep in here behind a closed door?" she asked.

"Because, I may have been good tonight, Mel. But I also have a bad side. And when it comes out, you'll need more than a flimsy door to hold me back."

Jesus, Johnny, and June, what have I done?

Aaron paced around the living room, cursing himself for what was by far the most idiotic move he could've made. He was acting like Cash again, thinking with his dick instead of his brain.

Not only did he spend his evening putting his hands all over that temptress who threatened to make him unravel, marking her like she was his, but then he went ahead and offered her shelter for another night. Or two!

Melody flippin' Sharp. Her name played in his brain, over and over again on repeat. It was musical and contradictory, soft and harsh at the same time. Much like her personality.

What the hell had gotten into him? The very last thing he should be doing was waxing all poetic about a girl who was just making a slight detour through his life. So they messed around a little. He didn't need to get all tangled up in her, that was for damn sure.

By tomorrow, he predicted, she'd be heading back home to Sweetwater. It was a thought that left a sour taste in his mouth for several reasons he couldn't explain and one he needed to expel—as in, *right the fuck now*. It was just…he hated to see her give up.

Though he could see her back in the fancy little town where men golfed on Saturdays and ladies went to lunch. Where you didn't lock your doors and would never be evicted from your home in the middle of the night, left with no place to go. The kind of place he once lived, before his dad died and his mama pissed away all of her money on booze and drugs and who knows what the hell else, forcing them to move from place to place until he finally got his own record deal and was able to send money home.

He stopped and picked up the one family photo he had sitting on the shelf with all of his music books, guitar picks, and strings. It was the only year he remembered all four of them together at Christmas—the year he got his first guitar. Mama tuned it for him and played carols all morning. It was the memory he always went back to as a kid, hoping it'd be that way again.

It never was.

If it wasn't for him and Graham, or his father getting sick, his mother might still be singing. The way he saw it, you had to choose. There was no room for a big career *and* a family.

His poor daddy learned that the hard way. Always alone with two little boys, while country sweetheart Corrine Mcadows was out "making music." Now that Aaron had been there, seen the lifestyle first-hand, he knew she was doing plenty more than that. She didn't come home, even when she had the opportunity. But his father never complained. He once told him that he knew what he was getting into with Corrine. Still, he wanted to be part of her life—even if it was a small part.

It was more than Aaron could say. He wanted nothing from her, or her pathetic life. Once he was able to afford to send Graham off to a private boarding school, he did. And during the holidays and breaks, the kid would come to stay with him. Even in the middle of the craziness, he always pulled it together for Graham. It was his job—though they never got the courts involved. They didn't have to, Corrine never fought his decision. For her, it was a relief to have someone else take over. Neither one of them had seen her since.

This is why you don't mix music with a family.

One would always suffer, and it was damn selfish to try to do both. He might not be able to stay away from playing his songs, but he could avoid bringing anyone else into the impossible lifestyle.

Shit, why was he thinking about this now? Must've been all the baring of the souls—and other, more interesting parts—with Mel tonight. It put him in such a state he wanted to drown his sorrows in a bottle of Jack. Instead he picked up his guitar, trying to put the night, and all the shit it dredged up, behind him.

Trouble was, the night also brought a spunky blonde with it, and so he couldn't put it completely out of his mind. Not when she was there, half-naked, in the next room. His depraved brain conjured up the way she looked when she told him she was going to come—her eyes hooded and lips swollen. The scent of her flushed skin, and the way it felt when she finally let go, was something he'd remember on his deathbed.

He played a few chords then, shutting his eyes to help quiet his mind. He'd never get any sleep unless he settled down, and he needed the rest in order to deal with his manager the next day. As his release date loomed, Rita became increasingly demanding. He had to be ready for her, and strong enough to draw the lines he required to keep his head straight.

But the sad truth was, as much as he loved cradling his guitar and hitting those soft low notes, that sorry plank of wood had nothing on Melody Sharp.

Chapter Seven

When Mel woke up, she'd forgotten where she was for a moment. But when she realized it was the cozy nest Aaron made for her, she refused to get up. How odd. She wasn't usually the type for lazy mornings in bed. She never really slept all that well...ever. Her mother used to say Mel was too busy for sleep, even as a child.

She wouldn't say busy, so much as unsettled. She rose most days already feeling two steps behind, like she was missing or forgetting something. Yet, that *something* never came to her. Last night, however, she went to bed feeling sated and, strangely cared for—the first time in a long while that she'd felt that way.

The sheets smelled like him, all woodsy and warm. She inhaled the intoxicating scent and reached her arms above her in a long, luxurious stretch, wishing he was there with her as a pale glow came in through the uncovered windows. She'd forgotten how much she missed morning sex, but she wasn't about to hunt him down and suggest it after he'd declined her multiple requests last night. Still, it seemed a shame to waste such a morning. So she let her anxious hand run down her belly, remembering the way he had touched her, kissed her, moved his fingers inside, bringing out a part of her that had been repressed for far too long. Her eyes fluttered shut when the tips of her fingers slid beneath the silky fabric…until she heard a floorboard creak.

Shitty shit shit.

She pulled her hand from the danger zone and shot up in the four-poster bed, eyes searching, fearful she'd been discovered. It was like high school all over again. There was no one there, but she wasn't taking any chances. She placed her palms on top of the covers where she could keep her eyes on them. Honestly.

After she found her breath, she took in the space that she'd been too preoccupied to notice the night before. It was identical to the room in her own apartment, but she used hers for an office. Here, boxes were piled high in the corner, a few family photos sat on the bureau, and a shelf of books and baseballs lined the far wall.

A knock on the door made her jump again. This time she was just relieved she stopped her trip down memory lane when she did.

"Come in," she called, feeling her face heat when a large cowboy wearing jeans and a T-shirt materialized in the doorway. He looked absolutely mouth-watering—his hair still wet from his morning shower, the sleeves of his shirt hugging biceps that she had the privilege of touching last night, and his jeans slung low on hips that she hadn't yet explored.

Yet. Hmmm.

She was so consumed by his presence she almost didn't see the massive cup of coffee in his hand. When she did, its rich aroma made her want to cry. "What time is it?" she asked, extending her gimmee hands for the java.

"Time for your sort to get off to work, I'd imagine," he said, passing her the mug.

The first sip was strong and smelled like toasted nuts and cocoa. Delicious. The caffeine went straight to her head, pushing her past the memories of her lust-fueled night with Aaron and her solo attempt this morning, to more pressing issues—such as her current homeless status, bank account balance, and mental state. Did she really beg a stranger for sex just a few hours ago? Yeah, she should probably be embarrassed by her behavior in front of the gorgeous man she'd only recently met, but she was already feeling too low from her current state of affairs to indulge in any further self-loathing.

Plus she liked him too damn much.

"Thank you," she said. "The coffee is perfection. And last night…"

"It's okay," he interrupted. "We don't have to talk about that. I was just being neighborly, is all." The corner of his lip turned up and amazingly made the awkwardness of the situation fade. *How did he do it?*

"Darlin', if the world had neighbors like you, we'd all live in a happier place." She flashed a quick wink. Yes, she really should be embarrassed. She clearly had not acted like a lady in her time of need. Still, Aaron looked down at her with a smile, so it couldn't have been all that bad. Could it?

She reached for her phone to check the time. He was right. She was due in the office in an hour. And then some more practical concerns seeped into her brain. She had no clothes, none of her things. What in God's name was she supposed to do now? Was it time to just call it quits?

No! The voice in her head was insistent. She needed to end her job at Elite on her own terms — on good terms. That way maybe could secure a good referral for a PR job close to home. Going back to Sweetwater with a plan would be a lot easier than just showing up at her parents' house, empty-handed.

"Well…" He headed for the door. "Let me know if you need anything."

She nodded, but all she really needed was the key to her apartment and her things. Just the thought of what happened when she went to her place last night had reignited the fire in her belly. She viciously punched her landlord's number into her phone, ready to unleash her fury.

Once he picked it up, she said one word. "Explain."

"Look, Mel," he told her. "I had no choice. You're two months behind in rent and you weren't returning my calls. My hands were tied. I have to answer to people as well."

"Of all the sneaky, lowdown, gutless moves," she hollered, good and loud so he was sure to hear exactly what she thought of him. "I was left alone, without a place to stay, in the middle of the night. In Atlanta. Who does that to somebody? Tell me that much, Cole."

"Like I said, my hands were tied."

"I told you about my pay cut. I just needed a few more weeks."

"That's what you said a few weeks ago." He released a long, annoying sigh. "Mel, I don't actually own the house, or the places downtown. I manage them for my parents and they are on my ass. I held out for you as long as I could."

A laugh crept up her throat. She knew it! God, she knew it! All these times he went strutting around like he was Mr. Big Shot Real Estate Mogul, trying to impress her before asking her out and then brushing her off when she said no, as if his options were endless. She always thought he was full of it.

"You know, Cole." Oh, she wasn't going to let him off that easy. "Before these last few months, I was never late. Never. Also, I think written notice is required in these situations. You can bet I'll be making my way down to the courthouse. And I'll be reviewing you—and your parents' company—on every social media site I get my hands on. Now, where are all my things?"

"Settle down, Mel." His voice wavered. "You don't have to do that. I took good care of your things, I promise. We shipped everything to Red River Storage on Axel Road. It's all in a unit and paid up through the end of the month. We can handle this without getting all nasty about it."

How generous.

She hung up on the bastard.

There was no chance of making it down there before work, so she'd have to get her stuff on the way home. But how to make herself presentable in the meantime?

"Mind if I take a shower before I go?" she called out to Aaron, who was messing around in the kitchen, if the clatter of pots and pans was any indication.

"Sure," he said. "There are extra towels already hanging in there."

She sized up her clothing options. Black tailored capri pants and the lavender blouse she wore yesterday, a scarf, a few pieces of extra jewelry in her bag, and a pair of flat-heeled sandals she always kept on her for relief when her feet ached from her crazy-high heeled shoes. Okay, she could pull this off.

After her shower, she wrapped her curly locks into a loose chignon and applied the makeup she never left home without—a survival plan she'd now used two times in as many days. She slipped into her black pants and pulled Aaron's white T-shirt over a camisole before cinching it with her pink scarf. She added a long pendant necklace and earrings to match, and slid into her backup shoes. A quick check of her reflection in the full-length mirror behind the bedroom door revealed she didn't look half bad.

Since the universe wasn't playing nice, today she would just have to start making her own luck.

What would Frankie do?

It was the question she had to answer if she was going to recover from this latest setback. What was Rule Number Three? *Connect and be connected; you don't have to go at it alone.* Okay, so who were her connections? Who could she reach out to in her time of need? There was Kevin, Tiffany the Intern, and her new friend Genn. None of them were great options, but these were desperate times. Once she got her things back, she could put them up on Craig's List to make a quick buck. And there were plenty of incentive programs at work that offered a pretty nice bonus. Point was, she had options.

Still, first things first—she needed to buy some time to

put some sort of plan in place. And hey, he'd offered…

She walked into the kitchen, rehearsing in her head what she planned to say. A place to crash for one night, two tops, was all she needed. She took a breath and put on her game face, but as she closed in, Aaron's words stopped her dead in her tracks.

"No, I haven't hired the party planners yet," he said into the phone, his voice quiet and clipped. She quickly backed out of the kitchen entry, behind the wall, to give him his privacy. "And as far as the image consultant, or whatever it is the label wants me to get, I'm not doing it." Well, those were words that made her ears perk right the hell up.

"The launch party will cost *how much?*" He slammed his hand down on the counter, making Mel jump. "That's not possible, Rita."

Holy shit! What was all this?

Aaron had a label? And a launch coming up? She tilted her head, holding the rest of her body still as she listened, riveted by the conversation. After his performance last night, she knew he was an incredible musician, but her brain was too focused on her own tragedy—and even more on his smoking bod—to give it another thought.

Was she really hearing this right? He needed party planners—an insulting term, but she'd let it go—and an image consultant?

"Hang on, Rita," he grumbled. "I'll ring you back in a few minutes."

He hung up and said a few choice words under his breath. On the other side of the wall, Mel began frantically typing on her phone. He came around the corner into the living room. He knew she was there, but she ignored him, holding up a finger to signal she needed a minute.

"What are you doing?" he asked when her fingers finally stilled.

"I'm getting ready to help out a neighbor." She put down the phone, grinning like Miranda on billing day. "So, you really need an event specialist and an image consultant?"

"Depends on who you ask." He shrugged. "If you ask my manager, Rita, well then the answer is hell yes."

"And you have a label?" she asked, her mind racing. This was huge. "As in *music* label?"

"I do," he ground out, running his hands through his hair. He swallowed and asked, "Why?"

"Why?" She laughed. "Because that's what I do, cowboy." She looked around the room for a pen and paper, finding what she was looking for on the built-in shelf leading to the kitchen. The notepad was full of notes and verses and random words. She flipped through it to a blank page, tore it out, and led Aaron to the kitchen table. It was already set with two place settings, and from the looks of all the pots and pans on the stove, he'd been making them breakfast when the call came in. His kindness only made her want to help him more.

"All right, I'll bite. What do you do?" he asked as she signaled him to sit.

"I work at one of the best PR firms in the country."

Cue the applause.

"Well, if you heard that much of my conversation. You also heard that I don't have the money to pay for PR or parties or fucking image consulting. Not sure your Ice Queen would go along with that."

"We could work that out if you're interested. Miranda

can be surprisingly creative with the accounting, if she really believes in someone. As for the imaging consulting, I have an idea."

"I appreciate that, honey, really I do." He set his phone on the table, like he was happy to get rid of it. Mel got the impression he didn't care for having to answer to someone. "But you told me yourself that you don't even know if you're going to stick around. And that your boss hates you. And a bunch of other crap that doesn't really scream, *hire me.*"

Ouch, the truth stung, but Frankie's Rule Number Two echoed in her brain. *Know what you want, and go for it.* She wanted this. She could do this. Turn this hunk-o-cowboy into a country music star? Yes, yes, for the love of Carrie Underwood, yes. She was made for this project.

Who was she kidding? *He* was made for it. That voice. That face. The way he looked in those jeans…and the way he *would* look once she shrunk those babies up in the right places.

"That may be true, but that was before this opportunity." She quickly jotted down her notes on the paper. "Elite is the best, Aaron. Even if something did happen with me — which it won't — you'd have a world-class team on your side."

"I can't afford the best." He leaned back in his chair and crossed his arms, defiant. "And I'm sorry, but I don't need — or particularly want — a launch party, and as far as the image consultant, I'm not some high-maintenance dipshit who needs all that crap. I signed with the label to play music and that's exactly what I'm going to do."

"That's all fine and dandy, but what about your contract?" She waited for a reply, but the look on his face, blank and confused, was all the answer she needed. He didn't have any idea what was in the contract, so she went in for the kill.

"There are all kinds of clauses and demands in most entertainment contracts that require marketing and appearances and an all-around effort on your part that goes beyond playing music. And if you think you don't have money now, breach that contract and we'll see how your finances are doing then."

His phone rang again and the screen flashed the name *Rita*. Aaron dropped his head into his hands. Now that lady had the kind of gumption she needed.

"Yeah." He answered on the third ring, but Mel grabbed the phone, put Rita on speaker, and set it back on the table.

"Jesus, Aaron," Rita said. "Is it so difficult to keep that phone next to you?"

Mel jotted one last note on the paper and pushed it in front of him. His brows furrowed as he read the words she wrote on the top of the page: "How to Build Your Brand."

"Earth to Aaron," Rita called out. "What is with you lately?"

"Yeah, yeah, I'm here," he said, looking up at Mel in question.

"Trust me," she mouthed to him, pointing to the diagram on the page, which was all about branding yourself for success. She'd done this with dozens of clients. Well, she'd watched her colleagues do it, anyway. By the time she got ahold of clients, they were already branded and ready to go, but it *was* her job to ensure the events that she coordinated were always in sync with the client's unique identity. And Aaron needed his in place before she made one call to plan the launch of his single.

"Look, I need to run something by you," he began.

Before he could finish, Mel rushed in and took over. "Hello, Rita," she began her introduction. "I'm Aaron's new publicist..."

"His *what*?" Rita said with a bite.

"I'm Melody Sharp with Elite Public Relations." Mel kept her voice clear and steady. She worked with the NFL, dammit. She managed events for actors and billionaires. Surely she could handle one music manager.

"Elite?" The bark had a little less bite. "As in, Miranda Well's Elite?"

There we go. "That's the one." Mel winked at Aaron.

"Oh, well, hello," she said, clearly shocked by the recent development. "I had no idea you were really on top of this, Aaron. But nice work. I approve of your choice, and the label will be thrilled."

Strangely, Aaron didn't seem that relieved and Rita... well, she couldn't get a read on her yet. But Mel paid them no mind. She was too busy figuring out what she'd have to do to convince Miranda to take Aaron on.

"I have a kickoff meeting with the rest of the team this morning," she lied. "So I'll get all of our paperwork and our plan for the launch to you just as soon as I can."

Funny, in all the time she'd been working at Elite, she'd never come close to lassoing a new client on her own. The staff was going to flip. And the way she planned to position her new find, there was no way Miranda would turn her down. She would make sure of it.

So this was what it felt like to take charge? Hmmm, she liked it. She liked it a lot.

Mel returned the phone to Aaron, gave him an enthusiastic smile, and stood up from the table. Then she walked over to the counter and plucked a piece of bacon from the plate Aaron had prepared, turning around to find him staring at her, mouth open and catching flies.

She took a bite of the salty delicacy, scooped up her purse and computer bag, and headed off to work. There was no time to waste. She had a visit with the Ice Queen to prepare for.

Chapter Eight

Mel walked into Elite early and paused at the fork in the office hallway, just as she had for the past month. Her feet stuttered every morning, ready to veer left to her old office. That's when her brain would kick in, remind her of all her past wrongdoings, and guide her to the right. She'd go, reluctantly, dragging her lifeless body the entire way.

Not this morning.

She practically skipped to Intern's Row—which, she discovered, was a ghost town at this time of day. Except for Tiffany the Intern. Dang, what was her last name?

"You're here early." She stopped at her cube and smiled, figuring it was time she stopped acting like the office bitch. That was Miranda's job.

"Mmm." The girl checked the clock on her laptop. "Same time as usual."

Mel leaned over her desk, finding her full name on one of the folders: Tiffany Williams. That was it. How rude she'd been sitting over here for the better part of a month and not once introduced herself. She couldn't do it now, it'd just be awkward, but she could change the way she treated her going forward.

"What are you working on?" Mel asked, watching as Tiffany fast-forwarded something that looked like news coverage on her computer.

"Sorry." Tiffany's cheeks turned pink as she quickly shut down the site. "My shift doesn't officially start until nine, so I was putting together my newsreel for school. Sorry, that was stupid. I won't do it again."

"Stop apologizing," Mel told her. "I was just curious. So you're good with video, huh?" Her mind started turning.

"I guess," Tiffany said, her tense expression fading.

Mel knew that meant she was very good. Girls like Tiffany didn't do things half-assed. They also underestimated themselves—she knew that first hand.

"Would you be interested in working with me on a project?" Mel asked.

The request had Tiffany up on her feet. "Sure." She said the words before Mel had explained what she needed. "Anything. What's the project?"

"Oh…" She studied her fingernails for effect. "Just the launch of the next Luke Bryan."

"Are you serious?" Tiffany picked up her iPad and began typing furiously. "What's his name? Where is he from? What do you want me to do first?"

"Well, *first* we have to sell the idea to the Ice—to Miranda," she corrected. "Got time to help me before the meeting?"

"Heck yes," she squealed, unable to control her excitement. "What do you need?"

"A complete audit on Aaron Major," she said. "We don't have a lot of time, but we have to jump on it now and I know very little about this man. I just found out about the project this morning, so I need all the extra hands I can get. Let's meet in the conference room in an hour to regroup."

"Okay, I'll be in the library if you need me," she said, gathering her supplies. "This is so exciting. I won't let you down, Melody. I promise."

Mel hoped she could say the same, but she was nervous about her proposition. Mel wasn't an initiator…not of anything, really. She was the person who took someone else's concept and ran with it. She was the cheerleader, the encouraging sideliner, the person who had your back. She was not the idea girl. Still, Tiffany's enthusiasm was catching.

As luck would have it, Thursdays were staff meeting days, where everyone would join together to discuss cases, issues, and opportunities. It would be the perfect time to pitch Aaron, but she had to be ready to anticipate her boss's every thought—her questions, her doubts, her overall disgust with Mel's past performance. Or worse? She had to consider that Miranda might like the idea, but might not trust Mel with it, and give it away to one of the other managers. If she wanted this, she'd have to make it clear that she was the logical lead for the case. She couldn't let it go to one of her former teammates. No. Matter. What. Being exiled to Intern's Row was tough enough. She didn't think she'd survive if Aaron's case went to someone else, especially The Weasel. So she'd have to be perfect, because Miranda was like an apex predator, able to sniff out the weak and always ready to move in for the kill

As she polished her pitch, an email address she didn't

recognize interrupted her, with the subject line: *Call Me*. What was it with these emails lately?

When she opened it, she was happy to find it was just Aaron's number. And that was a little embarrassing. Jesus, he'd given her the best orgasm of her life, all before they had the chance to exchange numbers.

"Hey," he answered on the first ring. "Rita talked to the Ice Queen."

"What?" Of course, his manager didn't trust her. Mel was used to that. Fine, if that's how she wanted to play.

"Sorry, but I can't control that woman," Aaron said. "But look, things went okay. I just didn't want to you be blindsided when you saw your boss."

There went her upper hand. Okay, but it wasn't enough to stop her. This time, her ass wasn't the only one on the line. She had Aaron to think about. She honestly believed in his talent, and she was confident Elite was the right place for him.

"Well cowboy, if you really want to help me, there's something I need you to do."

"Tiffany, I need your expertise with a video component for the meeting," Mel said as she walked into the conference room. "And graphics as well."

Tiffany was ready and waiting. "Got it, but you need to see this latest press about Aaron's comeback."

His what now?

Mel couldn't move as Tiffany delivered the news, blow by excruciating blow. Looks like Mr. Major had done this before. The bastard. Why didn't he tell her? He warned her about Rita, but had told her nothing about his own life of debauchery. And what really got her goat? She didn't do the checking on her own. She relied on an intern to do it for her. Still, she'd been busy researching the label, searching Elite's archives for other country 'launches' and scrambling to find successful debut examples. And hey, what did Frankie say? She didn't have to be the smartest person in the room. Just the most informed.

Okay, consider her briefed. Now she had an hour to prove it.

The next sixty minutes flew by in a blur of fact-checking and copy-writing and putting together a last ditch backup plan should it all go to hell. With ten minutes to spare, she reapplied her lipstick, tamed a few rogue curls from her updo, and took a seat next to Tiffany at the long conference table, sipping coffee while they waited until the team filtered in.

Those pitching always took a seat with the rest of the management, while everyone else stood. Just another protocol Miranda liked to use to make the staff uncomfortable. Mel didn't have time to rework her pitch to factor in the comeback, so she was going at it as if launching a new brand. She'd talk about the ugly backstory later.

It wasn't exactly as she planned. Still, she was ready.

But before she even had the chance to warm up her boss, Miranda came at her first thing once the meeting began.

"So, Melody." Mel hated the way Miranda said her name, long and drawn out, turning up the last syllable so it sounded like she was addressing a kindergartener. "I had an interesting conversation with a Nashville manager today, would you like to fill in the rest of the group?"

Miranda sounded nice. Too nice, and Mel worried she'd never get the chance to pitch her idea. Still, she'd told Rita that she wouldn't send over paperwork until the meeting. She hoped that bit of information made it into the conversation with her boss. Misrepresenting Elite was a surefire way to win her walking papers.

"Right." Mel set her shoulders and stood up. "I'm so glad you got the chance to speak with Rita this morning." Then she looked around the room at the rest of her colleagues. "I'm happy to announce I've found an opportunity for new business with an up-and-coming country artist."

She nodded to Tiffany, who passed out the flyers. She'd doctored up a factsheet that looked like a concert flyer to get everyone pumped up about the client. And from the expressions of all the ladies in the room, she'd killed it.

"Who is he?" Frederick asked, studying the photo. Shoot. She could see The Weasel's wheels turning. He was the office pain in the ass, and slicker than owl shit, always willing to sell someone out to get closer to Miranda.

"His name is Aaron Major and he's with Jumpstart Records," she said.

"Ah, Mel." Fredrick smirked. "That story's been done before. Aaron Major? Country music legacy out of West Texas makes good, heats up the charts, and then crashes and burns. End of story."

Mel embraced her inner Scarlett and prepared to take over the show.

Fiddledee fucking dee!

Returning Fredrick's smirk, she then turned her body in Miranda's direction. "Sure, I guess it'd be the end of the story, if he wasn't making music again, or hadn't secured a label, or didn't look like a cross between Luke Bryan and Jake Owen. Or if country music wasn't the number one music genre in the U.S.

"He was a baby when he debuted and let me tell you, I met with him this morning, and he is coming into this thing all man. New sound, new look. It's not a comeback story. It's a *taking the music scene by storm* story."

She took a sip of water and played it cool. But inside, her mind reeled. Not only about the freaking presentation, but about Aaron, too. She couldn't help it. He had been on top and had fallen from grace? No wonder he'd been so kind to her, so understanding of her pathetic sob-story and down-on-her-luck woes. He'd *been* there. He *was* there.

She didn't get the chance to dig into the past about his famous mama, but she did read that his daddy passed, and from the way it sounded last night, he kept close tabs on his brother. It made her want to help him. To fix this mess.

But why didn't he tell her? In her current homeless, quasi-jobless state, she wouldn't have been one to judge. That pang of hurt she felt because he hadn't confided in her—she squashed that down. She was swimming with the sharks in this conference room, and thanks to Frederick, her blood was already in the water.

"I don't think a washed up cowboy is worth our time," The Weasel continued. He was digging in and wasn't about to let it go. He loved watching people fail. The asshole all but helped her move her things to Intern Row after her demotion. At least he wasn't fighting for the project. That was a positive.

"That cowboy doesn't look washed up to me," the

director of media relations chimed in.

The hushed echoes of agreement started to fill the space.

She waited for the momentum of the room to take over.

"I don't think so either," Emily agreed, flashing Mel a wink. "And Jumpstart is making huge waves in Nashville right now."

Em led the Events group and tried to help when Mel was on the chopping block. She'd had a meeting with Miranda, but said there was nothing more she could do. Trouble was, nobody would ever cross Miranda. Mel understood. Life at Elite was easier when you weren't on the Ice Queen's shit list. But it was the way Em treated her afterward that really hurt. She'd pulled away from Mel and hadn't so much as looked in her direction since the demotion—which made her wary of her new found enthusiasm. Maybe *she* wanted Aaron.

God, it was painful just to think it. Then again, what if Em was the better person for the job? Could she take that away from him?

Not a chance.

Mel expelled a deep breath.

She'd make her pitch and do the best damn job she could, then she'd let the chips fall. She'd work her ass off for Aaron's campaign, but if Miranda thought there was someone better for the project, she wouldn't fight her. He deserved that much.

"He's the real deal, y'all." Mel lifted her chin and made eye contact with each person assembled around the vast conference table.

"Right." Fredrick rolled his eyes. "I don't care what you say. It's a comeback. Personally, I think people are tired of giving celebrities second chances."

She had planned to wait for this next part and do it privately with Miranda, when she told her about the tight timeline and the lack of budget. But Fredrick was pushing her into a corner—and at the moment, he had Miranda's ear. It was time for a new strategy.

"Okay, Fredrick," she conceded. "I understand where you're coming from. Thing is, Aaron Major is no longer a celebrity. He's just a guy who loves to play music." She nodded to Tiffany, who started setting up the screen at the far end of the room. "But I wouldn't expect you to take my word for it."

Tiffany dimmed the lights and hit play, and soon the only sound in the room was Aaron's sultry voice. She got Aaron to agree to a video stream from the apartment and Tiffany handled the rest. They'd recorded it and had it at the ready just in case the team gave her a hard time.

Damn, Aaron looked amazing on camera. Sure, he could stand a little polish, but all these guys were a mess coming up. Images of Blake Shelton and that unfortunate mullet flashed in her mind. But Aaron's chiseled features and his deep soulful eyes...whew. She gnawed on her lip, taking in the reactions around the room.

Once the impromptu concert was over, everyone but Fredrick and the Ice Queen broke out in applause.

Miranda, however, didn't say anything, or even move a muscle, for the longest time. She set her icy eyes on the screen and then on Mel and then back to the screen, her silky hair not moving an inch as she swung her head back and forth. Mel thought she'd explode.

"So he's the real deal, Mel?" Miranda pursed her lips

together and raised her brows.

The room grew eerily quiet. Everyone froze, too scared to say what they thought. But the hell with it—Mel had nothing to lose at this point.

"That's what I think," she said. "We go in, no apologies, no backstory. We start from scratch. Everything begins with the launch party, including the heavy hitters and key influencers in the industry. We rope them in with the music, and then Mr. Major will do the rest with his star appeal."

"And you think he has star appeal?" she asked.

Jesus, was the woman blind?

"He will when I'm through with him. So, what do you think?"

Miranda looked at her then, in a way that wasn't familiar. She looked…dare she say, *pleased*? "I think we want him. But who could take him on? That's the real question."

Mel swallowed the growing lump in her throat. It was do or die time. "I want this client, Miranda. I want to take the lead on the campaign."

The Weasel snickered.

Shit, the Ice Queen wasn't saying anything. Not a good sign. Time to backpedal. She would not screw this up for Aaron, so as much as it pained her to do it, Mel pretended to consult her notes and said, "Or, this client could be great for Emily's team."

"No, I don't think so." Miranda studied her phone. "Emily is preoccupied with Coca-Cola this fall."

"Okay," she said, moving on to second best. "Mindy's team would also be a good fit."

"No." Miranda said simply, offering no explanation as she shot that one down.

Pack up the bags, loser. It's time to go home.

Mel racked her brain. What other team could handle this? Who had the room in their schedule and was senior enough to take on a soon-to-be star? Nobody came to mind. She felt her eyes begin to fill. She was really hoping her pitch would put her back on the right track with Miranda.

Up on the screen, Aaron's face was frozen at the end of the video—him, and his shy smile that broke her heart. If Elite wouldn't take him on, what about another firm? Maybe Genn and her team of Neanderthals would sign Aaron. After all he'd been through, and all that he did for her, she wasn't going to leave him hanging. But Miranda answered those buzzing questions before she could.

"I was thinking *you* could take this one," she said, as if it were her own idea.

"Me?" Mel grabbed the chair afraid she'd drop on the spot. Hell yes, she'd play along. "I can do that. I already have a file going with ideas and have made initial calls. I'm ready to move on this whenever you are."

Was this really happening?

She almost dropped to her knees and offered up The Weasel as human sacrifice to the PR gods. She felt like she was being heard, for the first time in her career. And not because she was endorsing a colleague or cheering on her team. This was all her...and Tiffany. And Mel was going to be deserving of this leap of faith her boss was making with her, no matter how hard it was.

"Bring me the complete plan tomorrow, and we'll see whether or not I've made a mistake."

"Yes, ma'am. And...I'd like Tiffany on my team. She was instrumental in assisting with this presentation today."

"Fine, fine." Miranda left the room without any further discussion.

As soon as the door closed, Tiffany squealed, and most of the eyes in the room rolled in response. The girl was a squealer. Mel couldn't hold that against her. Plus, she felt like doing exactly the same thing.

"Nice work, Mel," Em said, and soon there was a crowd gathering around her just like the old days. And though a part of her wanted to tell the group they could take their fake complements and choke on them, she decided on the high road and opted for *thank you* instead.

That was different. What did they call this type of interacting? Oh yeah, adulting. Who knew it could feel so good? Still, she wasn't ready to go patting herself on the back just yet. Before she did one lick of work on Aaron's launch plan, she was going to have some words with her tight-lipped cowboy.

Chapter Nine

Aaron held his breath as he heard the clip-clap of shoes on the stairwell. In less than forty-eight hours, he'd memorized the rhythm of her walk. Mel's quick steps interrupted his train of thought, and he braced for the worst when she walked through the door.

He wasn't pleased with her earlier request. That's how she phrased it, *a simple request*, the she-devil. The way he saw it, she was forcing him to perform like a trained seal, begging for a spot in their circus act. No thanks.

The worst of it was he'd been edgy all day, worried they wouldn't like his music. The goddamn suits, who didn't know him from Adam. Why did he care? Why did he put himself through the hassle?

It was Mel, that's why. The woman had a way about her that had him reverting to a school boy—nodding and sayin' *yes, ma'am* to whatever she asked of him. Then there was Graham, and that kid never asked for a thing, never was bitter for the shitty hand he'd been dealt in life. And Aaron had the chance to make things better for him, with the help of some extra cash. He had to make this work, and if that meant going back to Nashville, well…

He didn't have to finish that thought, because that little blond darlin' had a smile on her face the size of his home state. He stood there waiting for her to say something. Anything. But she breezed by him, filling his head with the spicy, floral scent that almost made him forget about PR firms, and launch parties, and annoying managers.

Almost.

"So, Mr. Major, you didn't think to mention that this isn't your first rodeo?" She plopped on the couch and began unbuckling her sandals, which—on Mel—were just as sexy as five-inch heels. Damn her.

Yep, he'd known this was coming, but what was he supposed to do? Tell her his life story, the epic failure that it was, because she was going to plan a party for him? He winced thinking the words. Her job was more than that and he knew it. But he didn't need her going on about his botched career. He did enough of that on his own. So did Rita for that matter.

"You never asked." He sat on the couch next to her, easing her legs over his to help her with her shoes. It was too damn distracting watching *her* do it. And he'd been aching to get his hands on her again. "And really, how is it you didn't know, anyway?"

"I was in high school when you made it big, and was a little more interested in my college plans than what was going on in the country music scene."

"Don't you mean you were more interested in your

boyfriend's college plans?" There he went again. It was almost impossible to keep on his good behavior with this woman. And that kind of lashing out…well, that was just him deflecting. He needed to keep some kind of distance between them, and his asshole behavior was definitely one way.

"Careful, cowboy." She pulled her legs off his lap and rubbed her own feet. "You're sounding very close to the twat-waffle you used to be, and I'm this close," she held up her thumb and forefinger, "to closing your deal, with a delay in billing, mind you, based on the pitch that you've been *reborn*."

"Come again?" He scratched his head, unable to keep up, and he swore her eyes danced in delight.

"That's right," she stood up and wiggled her butt in a victory dance, which put him in the mood for his own version of celebration. "Miranda wants me to lead your cause. *If* I can sell her on the plan tomorrow."

"Your pitch worked?" He watched her glowing with pride, and it was a beautiful sight, especially after she'd been so broken the night before. So why was he worried? Her fire was back.

"It worked," she echoed, dancing her way into the kitchen.

"And they weren't freaked out about my crash and burn the first time out?" he called to her, thankful he didn't have to see her face when she answered. He hated thinking about what they said about him—all the judgment, deciding if he was good enough. It reminded him too much of his childhood, always trying to win the affection of his mama. And nothing was ever good enough to hold her attention for long.

"Sure they were, until I got hold of them…and they heard you sing." Now that was something he'd like to see. Mel and her hot temper coming to his defense. Shoot, he liked the idea of her in his corner. For professional reasons only…at least, that was what he was desperately trying to believe.

His refrigerator door opened and Mel shuffled around. She must be fixing something to eat. Food. Yes, that's exactly what he needed right now. He'd been so worried all day, he didn't realize how hungry he was, so he peeled himself off the couch and joined her.

"Point is…" She began pulling out lunchmeat and cheese and the few vegetables he had in the crisper. "If I'm going to do this, you have to tell me everything I need to know about the new Aaron Major. I could've made a fool out of myself if I didn't have that information before the meeting."

"But you did." He sidled up to her at the counter.

"Right, I did. Thanks to Tiffany the Intern. How does a sub sandwich sound?" She nudged him with her hip so he'd move down to give her some room.

Aaron pulled out the plates, bread, and a knife, and helped her stack the subs. "I'm sorry. I really am. It's just that I don't like talking about that time in my life. And honestly, I didn't think about giving you the heads up. You bolted out of here so fast, and when we talked on the phone, I was more anxious about Rita calling your boss."

Mel went rigid at the mention of his manager's name, which had him believing she might be an issue. What else was new? Rita most likely considered Mel a threat. She was used to being queen bee, because there'd never really been a female presence in his life. Rita liked it that way. And though he wanted to shake it off and assume her intentions were strictly professional, he wondered if it was more than that. Maybe there was some grain of truth to the words she'd once blurted in a drunken stupor long ago—when she confessed she was in love with him. She was completely shitfaced when she'd said it, which was why he never brought it up again. He had to admit, the possibility of her having feelings for him had given him pause before he contacted her about the new album. But hell, they had to be past it all at this point, right?

In the end, it didn't matter. He believed that it was better to go with the devil you know, and he knew what to expect with Rita. Anyone else would've been a crapshoot, and he couldn't handle the uncertainty this time around.

"You were anxious because you didn't think I could do it, right?" He caught a quick glimpse of the woman he tucked in bed last night, before she lifted her chin and busied herself with the sandwiches. He didn't like it one damn bit.

"Hey now." He placed a gentle hand on her shoulder and turned her to face him. "Don't do that. This is all new to me. Well, the 'reborn' part, anyway. I'm going to be a little on edge from time to time. You should know that about me if we're going to be working together."

"Okay." She visibly relaxed, and he realized he must've said something right. He wished he knew what it was. "Good to know. But your manager…"

Here we go.

"Do you think she was deliberately trying to blindside me?" Mel reached across Aaron's midsection to grab the mustard, and her scent made it hard for him to focus. He'd never get sick of the way she smelled. "You like?" she asked, holding up the mustard.

He nodded—for two reasons—then held up the jar of mayo in a silent question. She made a gagging motion. Okay, so no mayo for the belle.

"I'm not sure if she did it deliberately." He topped off the sandwiches and dumped a pile of chips on each plate. "I can tell you that she's not used to playing with others. Don't worry, I'll take care of it."

"It's not a big deal, but I'd like to know what I'm up against." She picked up her plate and ripped a few paper towels off the roll. "So what are the rules around here? Are we allowed to eat in the living room on really hard work days?"

"Hard days, easy days, doesn't matter. Mel, the only thing you need to know is that there are no rules." For her anyway. For him? There were a shitload. He cradled two water bottles in his arm before picking up his own plate.

"Sofa picnic, then?" She grinned.

"You've got it." Leave it to Mel to have a cute name for plunking their lazy asses down to eat dinner in front of the shiny box. Whatever. He was a fan of the sofa picnic.

But then, when he was good and full and content, she ruined his good mood. "Okay, now it's time to spill your guts, Major."

Awesome. That sounded about as fun as shoveling cow manure.

Being coy wasn't going to get him off the hook this time, but why give more than she needed? "What do you need to know?" Yep, they'd take it nice and slow—question by question.

"Birthday," she said and an iPad miraculously appeared

in her hands. This was her plan all along—ply him with food and steal all his dirty secrets.

"November fifteenth."

"Year?"

"1982."

"Where were you born?" She tapped away on her tablet.

"Amarillo, Texas," he said, bored of his own story already. "You know, I have a bio where you can get all of this stuff."

"I know." She grinned. "But I'm hoping as we talk you'll give me the good stuff. The extra stuff that's not already on Wikipedia. How about your family?"

"My mama was a country music singer, which I'm sure you've read about." He spit it out as fast as he could, like tearing off a Band-Aid. "My daddy was a working man, a carpenter, which I'm sure you didn't. He wasn't in the press much. He died when I was twelve. He was the best person I ever knew. And then there's my brother, Graham."

"I'm sorry about your daddy," she said, and he knew it was genuine. She was just trying to do a good job. "That must've been so hard for you and your brother. Where is he now?"

"Finishing up high school." Christ, the words hit him straight in the gut. How could that be already? He'd never tell his brother this, but he still saw him as that freckle-faced little kid with the goofy smile.

"You're close," she said, and he realized he was mugging a ridiculous grin of his own.

"Yeah, we're close. It's just the two of us now."

"Where's your mama?"

"Who knows? Once I got Graham into boarding school on the East Coast, she took off somewhere. We haven't seen her since. Graham stays with me over holidays and breaks."

Mel nodded and looked down at her notes. This was why he hated talking about shit. That look of pity. He didn't want or need anyone feeling sorry for him or thinking he was weak.

"Any exes I should be aware of?"

"Not really." How should he position this? He'd had plenty of women in his bed, but nothing serious. That was by design.

"So you've never been in love?" She was no longer going off her script. This was getting personal and it needed to stop. He hated dredging up the past, when he'd worked so hard to get beyond it. But he told Mel he'd be straight with her. She deserved it.

"There's only room for the music," he told her. "This business—the music thing inside me—is bigger than anything, anyone. Add in the money and fame, the people hanging on your every word and the women willing to do anything to be with you and it changes who you are. It changed me. I could never bring anyone else into that. So, no, I've never been in love"

"And now how do you feel about all that pressure?" she asked.

"Now? Hell, I'm probably risking my sanity again, just by trying to go back to music. But last year when I was about as low as I could go—depressed and miserable—I thought maybe, if I could keep the touring to a minimum and stay here, I could avoid the lifestyle. Still, it's no world to raise a family in."

"You've made your choice?" she asked, treading lightly for reasons he wasn't quite sure of. It wasn't like she was looking for something from him. She had her pick of men, one ready for her to come home. But if he didn't know better, he'd say she was disappointed. "You're officially off the market?"

"Yes, I guess if you put it that way. I've made my choice. Actually, I've set up rules to help me stay the course. No band, because they're trouble, full of drama, bad influences, and temptations, with little control. No Nashville, for the same reasons. And no extra distractions—like booze, drugs, relationships."

She was quiet for a long time before she looked at him and said, "That's pretty sad, that you lump love in with booze and drugs."

"Sad," he agreed. "But for me, I think one is as dangerous as the others."

So much for one easy question at a time. Still, he wondered how the hell she did it—got him talking and sharing all this junk from the past. This was the exact thing he'd been trying to avoid.

Mel hadn't even thought about what she was going to wear to work the next morning. Thankfully, Aaron had. Apparently he had a little chat with Cole while she was at the office, and miraculously, a bag of clothes from the storage unit arrived on his doorstep.

She was able to pull an outfit together, undergarments and all, though it pissed her off beyond belief knowing that Cole had sifted through her unmentionables.

Mel finished her presentation in the office the next

morning in record time, after about two pots of coffee, and was sure it was a winner. That, or sleep deprivation was diluting her judgment. She was up with Aaron until three a.m., badgering him with questions, because Lord knew he didn't offer up any information on his own. Stubborn wasn't even the word for it.

She had about an hour before her meeting with Miranda and needed one more set of eyes on the thing just to be sure, so she gave her new friend Genn a call.

"I did what you said." Mel thanked Genn for her suggestions with the Miranda situation, but quickly segued into the part where she desperately needed some of her help.

"Refresh my memory," Genn said. "We were a little lit up on Tuesday night. What did I tell you to do?"

Mel went through the play-by-play of what had happened over the past forty-eight hours, leaving out a few of the good parts that she wasn't ready to share yet. Genn was the perfect audience, cheering and gasping in all the right places. "Wow, I'm so impressed right now I'm practically speechless. When do you go in to see Miranda?"

"In an hour, which reminds me, do you have a few minutes to look at the presentation?"

"Of course. Send it over."

By the time she hit send, she had three interns—Paula, Kaye, and Will—mulling around her desk. After they saw what she did for Tiffany, she'd gained quite a following. It was Team Mel all the way. She put them all to work—she could use every free bit of labor they offered.

With their help and Genn's brilliance, Mel was ready to run into the lion's den. She was going to make Miranda's head spin. She'd practiced the presentation so many times she could do it in her sleep.

"It's time," Tiffany told her. "I've set up the projector in conference room three. Here's the clicker."

Of course, Miranda was already waiting for her. Intern Paula was following the Ice Queen all morning. Mel was not in the mood for any surprises.

Still, when she walked into room three, Miranda acted as though she was late.

Nice try, lady. There were ten minutes left on the clock.

"Melody," her boss sang. "I don't have all day, so let's go already."

"Aaron Major," she began without apology, and flashed her clicker to the screen to open the presentation. "The voice of country today."

She opened with the country music sales stats, popularity, and changing sound—all of which played to Aaron's strengths. Anyone else would've been impressed. It was an exciting and thorough beginning.

Yet Miranda circled her finger, telling Mel to keep it moving.

"This initial phase of the plan is short and sweet: it's all about his launch—pre and post event. We start building his brand with an online presence, get him going on social media, and create awareness in the press. Then we organize a huge record launch party at a famous spot in Atlanta with a multimedia invite to entice all the industry bigwigs. And we find two big-name artists to join Mr. Major on stage."

Hmm, it was such a nice name. Such a nice face. She wouldn't have any trouble getting the key players to stand up and take notice of him.

Mel went on to talk about the other plans: TV, maybe

even a cameo on a drama or sitcom. Morning talk shows or late night, where he'd perform. It wouldn't be easy, but she didn't want easy. Where was the fun in that? And not to be forgotten: radio, music blogs, podcasts, and a few well-placed leaks of the single.

"And?" The Ice Queen was lukewarm, nodding and tapping her blood-red nails on the table.

"And some perfectly timed drama," she added. "A budding romance with another hot up-and-comer. Or rumors of a romance. Or multiple rumors about multiple romances. Everyone loves a little outlaw in their country heroes, right? A little outlaw, but no cheating. That would have to be managed carefully."

Mel went over the tight calendar and then, ever so subtly, slid in the budget issues.

"He doesn't have the money for this?" Miranda actually laughed.

"It's a structured payout, when he hits certain goals, which he is guaranteed to hit with this plan. No different than what we do with fiscal year planning for businesses."

"But this is an expensive undertaking, Melody." She pursed her lips in a way that made her look like her skin was going to crack at any moment. "The multimedia component alone—"

"Will be done with the help of my intern," Mel said. "She's amazing, dependable, has the time, and is contracted with us through the end of the summer."

"But the media relations," she said, ticking off the areas of the plan, one by one, trying to poke holes.

Mel was ready.

She was certain that within a month, Aaron Major would

find a nice comfy spot at the top of the charts. It was like taking candy from a baby. There were only two things standing in her way: Miranda, and the current state of her cowboy. Right now he looked more like he should be working on an oil rig than melting ladies' hearts up on stage. Not that he wasn't gorgeous—he was. But it was hard to tell what was going on under all that hair. She considered herself damn lucky to know.

Yes, fans loved outlaw—but he best be a well-groomed one. The ladies went nuts for bedroom eyes, an all-American face, slim hips, and a hot ass covered in those tight jeans the country guys loved to wear—which, let's face it, left nothing to the imagination.

"Okay, Melody," she said, as if Mel was a child begging for an ice cream treat. "Let's see what you've got. But your pay is going to be on that, what did you call it? Oh yes, sliding scale."

"No problem," she said, hoping Aaron was going to be okay with the roommate situation for a few more weeks.

"And," Miranda stood and sauntered to the door, turning around at the threshold to throw poor, pathetic Mel a bone. "You can move back to your office for the duration of the campaign. After, we'll talk."

"That's okay," Mel said, packing up her own things. "I quite like where I am,"

At the moment, she really did.

Chapter Ten

For someone who didn't want all the goddamn publicity, he sure was acting like an attention-seeking whore, pacing around the apartment waiting for the news about his new publicist. So far he'd ignored four calls from Rita.

"Sugar, I've been doing some research," Rita said when he finally picked up the phone. "And I tell ya, maybe Elite isn't the right place."

"You said yourself that Miranda is the best." He kept his eyes glued to the windows. This point was moot, unless Mel got him in.

"Yes, yes, she is," Rita stuttered, almost as if Miranda Wells was listening in. "But who does she have on the account? This Melody Sharp? You've had a look at her, right? She's young, fresh out of school? That's what these big firms do sometimes—take on smaller, unknown clients, gouge them with fees, and put them at the dead bottom of priorities so the hacks can train on the job."

He bristled at the insult to Melody, and realized this was why he couldn't be happy for the news yesterday. Why he had to be such a downer. Rita helped make him this way, untrusting of anyone, unwilling to take a chance unless his manager orchestrated it. She pushed him down and showed him his place every damn time she had the opportunity. He fell for it. He'd let his insecurities take over and given her far too much control over him. But he wasn't wet behind the ears anymore, and while he appreciated her skeptical nature in some circumstances, and truly believed she had his best interest at heart, he'd be making his own decisions. This was his chance. His life. And he wasn't going to let anyone tell him how to live it, or step out of bounds, or fucking second-guess his decisions. That's what he needed to do—keep everyone in their own damn box.

He wasn't an idiot. Though he wouldn't want Mel thinking he didn't trust her, he'd done his own research. With everything on the line, he had to. Elite's reputation was unparalleled by any other firm in the industry—even in Nashville. And Mel's track record was much the same. She might've pissed off her boss, but her clients loved her. He made a few calls of his own to some people he knew with the Falcons. Once upon a time, he had friends on the team, and he'd sung the National Anthem on more than one occasion. And the front office sang Mel's praises. So did a few artists in the music industry.

So yeah, it was time to put his manager in her own rightful place.

"I appreciate your concern, Rita. But I've got someone on publicity and she'll take it from here. You just keep the lines of communication open with the label. Help me with your Nashville connection. I can handle things in Atlanta."

"But Aaron, I don't want you to get caught up in some girl's spell down there."

Right, because she wanted him to stay under hers. He had so many things he wanted to say at the moment, but he needed her. At least until his single dropped. If he could just get through the next three weeks…

"Don't worry about that. Just take care of your side of the business. That's what I need from you. Can you do that for me?"

"You know I can." She perked up a little. "As a matter of fact, I'm working on something as we speak."

"What it is?" He wasn't sure he wanted to know.

"You'll see," she sang. "I'll be in touch soon."

Then she hung up.

Mel better have this party and promotion thing buttoned up, 'cause Rita would make him pay for this if he had to come back groveling.

He went back to the song he'd been working on. It was starting to flow, and for once he didn't feel like he was bleeding on the page. It was almost…fun. By the time he checked the clock, a few hours had gone by. Shit, Mel should've been home by now.

He camped out by the back window to wait for her. It was another hour before she arrived, and when she stepped out of her car, she was dragging two bulging suitcases behind her. His stomach sank…until he realized she was bringing them in, not going away.

She did a victory fist pump when she saw him in the window. He rushed out to meet her.

"Why didn't you call me?" he asked, taking her bags.

"Because you're never by your phone. Isn't that what you told Rita? Anyway, I was too busy, and I had to pick up some essentials from my storage locker."

"Essentials, really? It feels like you have your entire apartment in here."

"I'm sorry. I know this is an inconvenience, but you're going to be thrilled with everything we have planned for you."

"So I'm in?" He stopped, and she smiled.

"You're so in," she said, setting her bags down. "And accounting will hold off on payment until your royalties are issued. We have you on a sliding scale."

He picked her up and spun her around. "And I'm not going to have to sell my soul to do this?"

"We'll see," she said jokingly, but it didn't help his anxiety about the whole thing.

They went through the details of the meeting with Miranda over pizza and beer. So far there had been nothing unreasonable. He was no expert in PR, but Rita had shared the proposal for the label's Nashville agency a while back, so he used that to compare the costs. The billing was really all he could go on because the rest of it was in a language he'd never understand. But if he could keep the overhead low on this project, he might actually come out of this thing cheaper than if he'd done everything in Nashville. He was relieved, happy to do the work to make this part of the launch a success.

More than anything, he trusted Mel. But now that the campaign was underway, and she was going to be staying with him for the better part of a month, there were some new problems they'd have to deal with. Like her wicked scent, which flooded his brain whenever they shared the same space. And all that creamy skin, peeking out from her shirt. He knew he liked it far more than he should.

He needed to put her in the business box, and set the boundaries just like he was doing with Rita. Still…

"When do we start?" he asked her, hoping he had some time. One last night before their official relationship was, well, official.

"Tomorrow," she said, pulling out the paperwork. "Once you sign these."

Perfect.

"In that case…" He pushed the papers off the table, grabbed Mel, and deposited her on top of it in one fluid move. "We have just enough time to get this in. Because, honey, I won't be able to think straight until I have one more taste of you."

The rise and fall of her chest made him instantly hard; he could only hope she felt just as turned on. He'd touch her like this one last time and let whatever it was between them work its way out of his system. Then it was back to business.

Careful to brace his weight, he leaned over her, tracing the shell of her ear with his tongue. "I want you, Mel. I want you bad."

He nibbled his way down her neck, and then looked up for permission. Her parted lips and soft eyes were exactly what he was hoping for, and he wasted no time covering her mouth with his in a searing kiss. She opened to him, no questions asked. And this time, he let *her* touch. Her hands dove in his hair, held his face, slipped under his shirt. He felt her everywhere. The connection was undeniable. Their mouths melded together, their centers aligned and they moved in sync until she put her hands on his chest to stop.

He froze instantly, even though it was painful to move away from her. He'd never wanted anything—or anyone—more.

"You said the other night was just a one-time t-thing," she stuttered, her eyelids heavy.

"I also told you I have a bad side, Mel. And this tight little body brings it right the hell out. So you tell me now if this is something you want."

Her hands snaked around his back, and she pulled him to her. "I want."

That's all it took. He dragged her shirt over her head and descended straight to that tiny space between her shoulder and neck, where that Melody-scent was the strongest. He pulled the tie from her hair, fanning the impossibly soft tresses over the table. She was a picture. He nipped and sucked his way across her skin, nearly ripping the pretty lace bra off her pert breasts in the process. Her groans, and the needy little shifts she was making below her waist, said he was doing something right. It made his movements even more intense as he tweaked her pink nipples to tight peaks.

He wanted more. Sliding her skirt up around her stomach, he took a second to appreciate her matching panties before he tugged them over to the side. Damn. Feeling her last night almost did him in, but seeing her in the flesh, with all that soft skin? His entire body vibrated as he fought to hold himself back.

He pulled her to the edge of the table and slipped two fingers inside her wet heat.

"Ah," she cried out, reminding him that he had to go slow.

"Condom," Mel gasped. "Get a goddamn, fucking condom."

Or not.

He adored the mouth on her, focusing on her dirty words rather than what she was really saying.

"Condom, Aaron, please." She sat up and reached out, holding his face in her hands, so there was no mistaking the urgency.

"Fuck me," he grunted, before slowly pumping his fingers inside her.

"That's what I'm trying to do," she replied, undoing the button of his pants and sliding those greedy hands inside. "Now be a good boy and find me a little foil packet that says we can be bad...for just one night."

"I don't have any," he blurted, in what was sure to be a mood killer. *Stupid, stupid, stupid*. He'd had all day to prepare. Not that he was planning this, but still...what an idiot.

"No. no. no." He watched as her expression soured. Her face was flushed, wild, gorgeous. Then she wrapped her fingers around his hard-as-steel length and stroked him from root to tip, a little rougher than he expected. He wasn't worried; he could take anything she had to dish out. He welcomed it.

"So you're going to punish me, is that it?" He increased the tempo of his own fingers, doing a little disciplining of his own.

"You got that right, cowboy." Her voice was low and breathy. Sexy as hell. She touched him again, but this time, it was more of a caress as she reached the crown of his cock and glided her thumb through the bead of liquid at the tip, spreading it over him.

"So, we do this high-school style, then?" His breath grew

shallow and he had to fight to get the words out.

"Mmm," she groaned as they continued their assault on each other. "What's that?"

"I do you," he rasped. "And you do me."

"Okay." She tightened her grip and he thrust his hips into her hand. "But together. At the same time." She offered a level of intimacy he didn't deserve, but he took it nevertheless.

"Together," he repeated, his hand picking up speed as she began to open a little more for him with each thrust. He was getting to know her body, learning all the good stuff. How the hell was he going to stop after tonight?

They moved, so completely responsive to each other's touch. Though their position was a little clumsy, a bit uncomfortable. Mostly it was hot as fuck, and soon their hands worked each other into a frenzy.

He met her stroke for stroke. She was so wet, so close, but he left her teetering on the edge. She did the same… until he began to throb and she clenched around him. It only spurred them on, as if it was a contest of who could get the other off the fastest.

He won. Just barely.

Chapter Eleven

Mel sat at the kitchen table, drinking her coffee, feeling unsettled. Yes, she'd agreed to Aaron's proposal: one night together before the contracts were signed and the PR campaign was underway. They'd get it out of their systems, and it'd be strictly business between them after that.

Turns out, it was the most amazing sexual experience of her life. But it wasn't enough.

She leaned sideways to peek around the doorway and watched as he tinkered with his guitar, wearing his uniform of T-shirt and jeans. But this morning he also had bare feet and bedhead—an irresistible combination. It took all her willpower to stay put and not go out there and jump the man's bones.

When she accepted his suggestion, she truly thought it'd take care of all the sexual tension, freeing them to work without distraction. It only made it worse. Especially when they'd yet to seal the deal. She hated to think it, but really, what kind of musician didn't have a king-sized box of condoms in his home?

She was glad—thrilled actually—that he didn't. Still, she'd been hoping for the complete Aaron Major experience. She should've negotiated a better deal.

Frankie Fink would not be pleased.

There was nothing she could do about it now. She agreed that they should keep things professional from this point forward, and she respected his rules. Plus, they had work to do. Or she did, anyway.

She spent her Saturday filing the paperwork, working with Tiffany to set up Aaron's social media accounts and get his website up and running. The design team had templates for situations like this, so she only needed an intern to customize the basics. Tiffany had been a godsend. So Mr. Aaron Major was back in the game. After all, if his every move wasn't accounted for on social media, it simply didn't happen, right?

Once the evening rolled around, it was time to work on the branding so she had to track him down. Like it or not. It didn't take long to find him hiding out with his guitar on the porch, probably trying to avoid her.

"Hey." She took a seat next to him.

"Hey, yourself," he said continuing to play.

"That sounds good. Really good." She could listen to him play music all day, every day. He was so soulful and…

Control yourself, Mel.

"It does?" He winced.

"Of course. You can't tell?" She slipped off her shoes and tucked her feet up on the chair. She wanted to get him talking, not just for the work. She really wanted to know about him and his life.

"I used to think I could," he said, "but ever since I left Nashville, I've been second-guessing everything. I'm not sure I do know what's good anymore."

Looking at him on the front porch with a guitar in his lap and the sun beginning to set behind him, it was hard to believe he ever had any doubts.

"What about your single?" she wondered aloud. "You must've been confident about that one. Especially to get Rita involved again."

"Yeah, you're right. I did know, but it took a year of picking the hell out of it before I was ready."

"What did you do when you were with the band? You had albums coming out continually." When she'd done her research, she was amazed at how much work they'd pumped out in a fairly short period of time.

"That was our guitar player, Jayden Jones, not me." Hmm, she noticed that his voice changed when he said Jayden's name.

"I find it hard to believe that you didn't contribute at all. Don't get me wrong, but you seem to be a little bit of a control freak." Images from the night before began to flip through her head.

"That's me now." He laughed. "Back then I didn't give a shit."

"Okay." She pulled out her iPad. "Tell me about the artist you'd like to be now."

"Do you always use such a clean segue? You seem to have a knack for them."

She wasn't going to answer that. "I do have a branding document I'd like to work on."

"What do you need, Sharp?"

"Since you've asked," she said, watching as he rolled his eyes at her. "I need you to fill out the form, and Tiffany and I will take care of it tomorrow afternoon."

She left him to it. But it was hard pinning Aaron down on the type of artist he wanted to be. The only name he'd given her was Casey Black, and that man was older than dirt. Not really the best example for his demographic. Still, Aaron didn't want to be lumped in with any of today's modern stars. And as he was so fond of saying, "I'm a person, not a household cleaner. I don't need a brand." She let him believe it.

For what she had planned, it might be easier that way.

Chapter Twelve

Mel stood in front of Aaron, taking in every delicious inch of him. D-day had arrived, and she was about to turn this lumbersexual into a country star.

"So what do you know about image consulting anyway?" Aaron asked as he wiggled around in the chair that Mel set up for him in the kitchen.

"Please. Do I really need to give you my resume when it comes to making things nice and pretty?" she asked, smoothing down her favorite dress.

"No, gorgeous. But I'd like to know what kind of *images* you've worked on in the past. Are you going to try to get me to wear purple jeans or put me in a fedora or some shit? Because I'm telling you right now, there are only two kind of hats I wear—cowboy and baseball—and that's it."

"What in the hell are you talking about? I'm not going to put you in purple jeans." The fedora, however... She did have a Jason Mraz-ish page in her look book. Last night when she was trying to stay put in her bedroom, she put together all her thoughts on his look and brand. This was going to be fun.

"I just want to know what I'm in for," he growled.

"You're in for a good time, and if you behave, we can catch the Braves game and enjoy what's left of the weekend.

"Just look at this." She gestured to her own immaculate hair and makeup to further illustrate her point. Of course, she would only say such cocky words to him. Because he got her, she didn't have to use her filter around him. And it was true—she was a master at making things, and people, look good. "What more do you need to know?"

"So you know how to dress, and yes, you are a freak of nature. The perfection of all this…" He waved a hand in her direction. "But how does that translate into other people? What are you going to change me into?"

"It's not about *changing* you, sugar," she said. "It's about helping you feel more comfortable in your own skin. Making you own who you are. When people look at you, we want them to see and think: *country star*. We want you to command respect with a glance. And you are a star. Now, it's time everyone else knows that."

"I *was* a country star, Mel," he said. "And that was a long time ago. Now I just want to make music so I can make a few bucks."

"You were a wild kid with too much money and too much fame before you were ready," she corrected. "This is why your image is even more important now. You have the outlaw past, which country music fans love, but we need to warm you up. Let them see the softer side of you. And a little more sex appeal wouldn't hurt either."

"I don't like the sound of that." He gritted his teeth, his eyes already gone stone cold.

"Baby steps, cowboy," she crooned. "Baby steps. But back to your question—I helped my sorority sisters land internships with Fortune 500 companies. Two of them are now on the Top Thirty Most Influential Business Professionals Under Thirty list"

"Atlanta list?"

"United States' list, smart ass. And those were just friendly tips. At Elite, I've polished up some of the best and brightest in entertainment, sports, and business."

"Anyone I know?" He looked up, all wide-eyed and innocent. She had the feeling he knew more than he was letting on.

"Like I'd tell."

"I could make you." He clamped his hands around her hips.

"This is a high-security vault." She tapped her temple. "No way you're getting in. Okay, time to be serious. Is there anything you need or want before we do this? One last photo of your hair or something to hang onto, other than my hips, when I start cutting?"

"Are you shitting me?" he said, releasing a loud *pfft*. He could be such a child.

"Not at all," she told him. "This can be emotional. People cry all the time when they cut their hair. And look at you. The long locks, your facial hair… It's hot, don't get me wrong. But it also seems like a bit of armor. You've been in hiding, Aaron Major, and we're about to reintroduce you into the world. Are you ready?"

"No." He rolled his eyes. "But don't let that stop you."

She started with his hair. Mel hadn't gone to school to

be a stylist, but no one would ever know it. All throughout college she took care of the girls who didn't have money for salon appointments, and took care of most of their fraternity brothers as well. Still, her hands shook a little. He was so gorgeous, she couldn't mess this up. And she couldn't trust anyone else with the job. She knew what he needed—she could picture it in her head. He still needed his crowning glory. The man had the best bed hair, the kind women would wanted to dig their hands into while he was... She didn't want to go there. But that's what the ladies would see when they looked at him, and it was her job to deliver that fantasy. Right now, it was too unruly, too harsh. She needed to soften his image without taking away the outlaw. The perfect combination of naughty and nice. Just as she pitched him at Elite, a little Jake Owen mixed with Luke Bryan. But better.

There was something oddly intimate about cutting his hair. The close proximity. The touching. Lord, the touching. She took slow, deep breaths to keep it together. To keep from wrapping her hands in those locks and giving a little tug. Oh, how she wanted to tug. And there went her nipples, joining in the fun.

How was she going to get through this campaign? Three weeks of fawning over this man. This quiet cowboy who she knew had a darker side. A wild side he'd shown her that first night she stayed with him, not to mention all the deliciously dirty things they'd done on the kitchen table. But he had been restrained ever since. She wondered if it took effort, or if he just didn't find her all that appealing. After all, she knew she wasn't sexy. She was the girl that guys liked to bring home to mama, but not the kind to warm their bed. She was everything he didn't want. Safe. Put together. Predictable?

She effing hated that.

"So are you going to do it, or just play with my hair all day?"

"Hush," she said, allowing herself one little pull after his snarky comment. As she did it, she felt her own little tug... right between her legs. She swore she heard him hiss.

"Dude, your hair is one of your biggest assets, and I don't want to fuck it up," she told him.

"Do I need to remind you that it's not even close to my biggest asset?" he asked, his voice low and throaty, making her wet. Damn him, making her think about all his assets!

She let the comment go, hoping she'd get to see that for herself before this arrangement was over. She steadied her hand and started cutting.

The first thing she did was take up the length, combing it straight down past his broad shoulders, where it landed right between the blades. She pressed her hand against his strong back, gathering his hair between her finger tips, and made the first snip. Again. And again.

She held a handful of the long locks in front of Aaron, who finally expelled the breath he'd been holding.

"Hard part's done," she said, while he ran his hand down to the cut that ended in the middle of the nape of his neck.

"No shorter," he barked, snagging her wrist in a motion that had her skin peppering in goose bumps.

"Don't worry. We don't want you looking like you're going to a board meeting. I just need to shape it now. No more off the length."

"Okay," he said, releasing his grip on her.

She went to work creating long layers that hung perfect-ly. The guy had a nice skull. The fact that she found even the shape of his head appealing was a little more than disturbing. She was so screwed.

She pulled around to the front of him, a finger under his chin to lift his head. The goal was to frame his face, showing off his eyes, but also concealing them when his hair fell a certain way.

"Shake your head," she told him and his hair mussed stylishly. She'd killed it. When he took the stage, the women were going to lose their ever-loving minds. "Okay, we're ready to tackle the scruff."

"I don't do clean shaven."

"Understood," she said. He had no idea how much he'd be thanking her by the time she was done with him. "I'm looking more for 24-hour shadow. Rough and sexy without trapping your lunch inside."

"Hey." He was clearly insulted. "I'm not one of those hipsters who conserve water. I shower regularly and do not let my beard become a petri dish."

"Still." She prepared the hot towels and razor. "I want to be able to see the line of your jaw. As a singer, all eyes will be on your face, on your mouth especially, and we want the audience to be able to see it. So you're going to have to bear with me. One clean shave and then once it grows to the perfect length, we'll just trim it as needed."

"You know I don't give a rat's ass about my image, don't you?"

"I've come to realize that, yes, but your agent does. Your label does. So I do, too."

Mel thoroughly enjoyed every second of handling Aaron Major, gripping his chin to turn his face in the direction she wanted as she held a razor to his face.

"Why do I get the feeling you're enjoying this more than you should?"

"I just like to make things pretty, that's all."

"See!" He slammed his hands down on his legs, forcing Mel to jump back before slicing his jugular. "I don't want to be pretty."

"I didn't mean it literally, tough guy. You look just as masculine as you did under all that hair."

"Honestly?"

"Girl Scouts' honor," she said, keeping her eyes on his lips. "Let me finish."

Mel needed complete concentration as she tackled the area by his lips. His plump irresistible lips. Her thumb traced the bottom one, feeling for stubble. Aaron separated them, slightly, and her knees went wobbly.

She couldn't let him know about that. This was her last chance at being able to stay in Atlanta. Her only chance. She couldn't blow that, no matter how badly she wanted to ride this cowboy. She wouldn't risk it.

Thankfully, Aaron's phone went off, providing just the distraction they needed.

Aaron flipped his phone around, so Mel could see Rita's name in bold letters.

"Let me deal with it," Mel said. The woman had been calling non-stop since Mel sent over all the material, but Aaron wanted to freeze her out for a while. It was a control thing, but it was time to put an end to it.

"You don't have to," Aaron said. "Who I hire is my business." He had filled her in on his last exchange with Rita, and though Mel loved his appreciation of her PR role it wasn't smart business to piss off his manager.

"Yes, that's absolutely true," she agreed. "But I need her. We need the whole team all-in on this. Why don't you take a shower? You have to be itchy from the haircut and shave. I'll make nice with Rita."

"You don't have to make nice." He was stern, protective, and it had her nipples tightening under her shirt. *Real professional.*

"Okay then." She crossed her arms over her chest in an effort to conceal her inappropriate reaction. "I'll update her on the plan and see if she has any questions."

"Rita, it's Mel," she said as she picked up the call and shooed Aaron away. For once, he listened, slinking away to the bathroom. "Aaron's not here right now, but I wanted to talk to you. See if you had any questions with the campaign."

"Oh, Mel, hello." Rita sounded irritated. "Don't worry about it. If I have any questions, I'll go to Miranda."

Do not let her bait you.

"Unfortunately, that's not how Miranda works." Mel kept her voice even, struggling to keep any defensive vibe from her tone. She was beginning to detest this woman, and was sick and damn tired of people trying to steamroll over her. "Day-to-day work and questions are handled by the account lead. Plus, Miranda is traveling and unavailable for the next week."

"Well then, I can always chat with Aaron."

Oh, hell no.

"As I'm sure you know, bothering an artist with the marketing and promotion is not good for him. Especially as he prepares for the launch and continues to work on his album."

"Look, Mel, while you were dealing with pimples and

deciding who was going to deflower you, I was managing Aaron Major's career. I hardly need assistance in that area."

"Are you sure about that?" Mel fired back. "Perhaps if it was done right the first time, we wouldn't be in this mess. Look, I don't care if you like me or respect me. But, I do need your cooperation and assistance—with the label, with the attendance list for the launch…with anything that will make all of this easy on our artist. Or don't you care about that?"

"That's the only thing I care about."

"Good. Then I'll email you an update on the latest progress, along with a few notes that I need you to answer… by the end of the day."

Rita agreed and then simply hung up.

Aaron was back in the very next moment. He must've been worried. She wasn't. In fact, she handled the situation better than she would have expected. "How was it?" he asked, towel-drying his hair.

She pulled the towel away from him and took over the job, running her hands through his hair one more time…just because she could.

"It was fine," she told him. "You don't have to worry about us. We'll play nice, I promise."

"It's not you I'm worried about, darlin'."

There was always something about holding a guitar that put Aaron at ease. Like a toddler's pacifier, it was comforting. There was never room for doubt or stress when he played. Even when things went down the shitter the first time around, he never resented the music. Not once. No, that was best saved for the people who set him off on the wrong path. His manager, the band he opened for, the long and willing line of women who were too available.

And there was another lie.

He was to blame. Nobody else.

Mel snuggled in on his couch—which he noticed now was decorated with fancy blue pillows—waiting to see him in action. He had unpacked, mostly. All the boxes were out back, waiting to be recycled. He'd been so busy he hadn't realized that his place was starting to look like more of a home. As he took it all in, he found more items that weren't his, yet seemed to belong in the space. When did she have time to do all of this? A simple painting hung on the wall behind the couch. Some sculpture thingy sat on his coffee table. Coasters, books, lamps, art were scattered about. It was subtle, but it was there. A woman's touch. Yes, Mel did know how to make things pretty.

"Where'd all this stuff come from?" he asked, tuning his guitar.

"Just a few things from my storage locker," she said with pride as she looked over the room. "I thought you might feel more at home if this actually felt a little bit more like a home."

"I do," he said, pulling out a kitchen stool to sit on.

And then he started to play.

She made him go through his three songs and he wasn't sure if she should be honored or insulted. Did she enjoy it, or was she critiquing him, waiting for it to get better?

Her expression was guarded, and he didn't like it one bit. That first night, she'd held nothing back from him. That all changed once they'd started working together. From the moment he'd signed that contract, he sensed ulterior motives and other things at play. There was no more sharing from her. She only wanted to know about him. It was all about the campaign. Sure, the chemistry was still there. That was just sex, nothing more. And now that was off the table, too, so to speak.

That was a damn shame, because going at it high school style with Mel was hands down the best time he'd ever had with anyone. But damn, if she knew how hard it was to leave it at that. As soon as the dust settled from their romp on the table, all he could think about was rushing to the drugstore for condoms. But he didn't want to scare her off.

They'd agreed on one time, and he didn't want to give the impression he was a horny old man. If he'd really been thinking with his head, instead of other more demanding body parts, he would've worded his proposition a little differently.

It was for the best. It was in the best interest of both of their careers to keep their distance. He had his rules for a reason. He'd suffered one breakdown. He didn't think he'd survive another.

The business of making music was starting to fuck with his life the second time around, and it was pissing him right the hell off.

He finished the set and tried to determine what was going on inside that pretty head of hers. She didn't make him wait. Her face broke into the smile he was becoming addicted to, the one he was willing to do most anything to coax into an appearance.

"That was so, so great, Aaron." She clapped her hands together, clearly pleased with him. Or was it the work she'd done on him? "Aching and angry, sad and desperate, and hotter than sin in all the right places."

He wanted to tell her that was her doing, but he thought better of it. "So now what?"

"Now," her grin widened, if that was possible. "We turn on the Braves game and relax. We deserve it."

"You like baseball?"

"No." She grabbed his guitar and placed it on the stand. "I fucking love it."

Shit, she had to go ahead and say that.

Chapter Thirteen

Mel flipped through almost a week's worth of mail, waiting for Aaron to wake up. That man kept some crazy hours. In her boredom, she took a chance to see if her magazines were still being delivered to her mailbox. She was pleasantly surprised they were, along with all of her personal mail. Dumb-ass Cole hadn't sent notice to the post office yet, so she was still getting past due notices and brand new bills to her former address. Oh, and the official invitation for the Sweetwater's Last Hurrah. Not that she'd forgotten about her hometown party. Or Teddy's surprise appearance. But the letter sure did put a timestamp on the festivities. They were now T-minus twenty-one days and counting.

She no longer knew how she felt about all of that. Not after spending the better part of the weekend with Aaron. Not to mention a serenade that could've charmed the panties of a nun. Yes, she had underwear on the brain, but it wasn't her fault the man channeled all her thoughts to below the

waist. She was obsessed with watching him play and sing…
and cook, surf channels on TV, or anything, really. Yesterday,
she asked for song after song until she was burning with
so much need her skirt was ready to start on fire. Then she
watched baseball with him—as it went into extra innings—
before she was finally able to high-tail it to bed.

Frustrated again.

And speaking of frustrating, she had to call Viv and deliver some bad news. Miranda had really trusted Mel with
Aaron's project, and it was going to take every free minute
she had to make it a success. So there was no way she could
take time off to see her friend that upcoming weekend.

"Vivi," Mel said when her friend picked up the phone. "I
have some bad news."

"Uh-oh. What is it?"

"I'm so sorry, but I can't make it this coming weekend."

"What happened?" Viv asked, in a sad tone that broke
her heart.

"Long story," Mel told her. "But I have a huge new
client, and Miranda's on my ass like you wouldn't believe.
All this talk about going with my instinct, and commitment
to my career, and blah, blah, blah."

"Who is the client?" she asked, sounding suspicious.

"A country artist, actually," Mel said with a quiver,
thinking about last night.

"Mmm-hmm," Viv said. "And what does this country
artist look like?"

"Oh, I don't know." A nervous laugh fell from Mel's lips.
"Like a cowboy, I guess."

Busted.

"Well, you be careful with that, hon," she said. "I've

heard cowboys are even more dangerous than race car drivers."

Mel pouted a little when she hung up. She desperately needed that time away with Viv. The two of them had endured so much with the Ice Queen—and just life in general. Nobody could possibly understand what it was like to navigate through the Miranda Wells landmines of double talk, snide comments, and criticism disguised to look like she was doing you a favor.

No, she needed Viv and needed her bad. Her friend was brilliant, driven, and resourceful—if anyone could help her, it was Vivi.

Plus, Viv had gone through her own crisis with a client—one who eventually became her fiancée. Not that Mel expected the same turnout. Not. At. All. But she might have some tips and tricks to getting out of this situation unscathed. Then again, if Viv knew how strapped Mel was for cash, she'd never let it go. And Mel wasn't taking handouts.

Her situation, with Aaron? Not a handout. It was a totally different work-for-room-and-board type of thing. That was perfectly acceptable. And let's face it—he was getting a major break with the delayed billing she'd secured for him. It wasn't a one-sided situation.

But if he wanted to make good on their contract, he needed to start the day with the rest of the world and not on music star time. It was time to move. She was on parole from the Ice Queen today to work with the cowboy. And if they were going to make the first meeting, she needed to drag his sweet behind out of bed. Pronto.

"Rise and shine, sleepyhead." Mel invaded his room at the first sign of daylight shining through his window. Dawn was an obscene time of day he chose to ignore.

"Nobody's home," he barked. "Come back later." Aaron was up most of the night writing a new song. He'd been pouring his heart into his comeback and left nothing on the table. But last night, he breathed new life into his work.

He didn't want to think about the possibility that it was Mel who brought the inspiration. And he definitely didn't want her pulling him out of bed after his all-nighter. He whipped the sheets over his head and tried to ignore her.

"This is serious music business," she said, inching her way closer. He could hear her light footsteps, and hell, her damn spicy scent was wafting its way under his sheets.

"Stop right there," he threatened.

Another step.

"I mean it, Mel."

Another step.

Then silence.

Until she gripped the sheets and pulled.

"Oh my God," she screamed. "Sorry. Sorry. Sorry." She was babbling now. Served her right.

Yep, he was buck-ass-naked. And though he'd already made her come—twice—and she'd returned the favor, she'd never had a chance to really look at the goods before. She'd touched him—oh boy, had she touched him—but seeing him in his glory in the light of day, first thing in the morning? Clearly not what she expected.

He chuckled. "I warned you, Mel."

"I didn't think," she said, flipping the covers back over his now wide awake body when he made no effort to cover himself. "Do you always sleep naked?"

"Always."

"And do you always wake up *that* way?" she asked, always so bold with her questions. He loved that about her.

"Always," he said again.

"Well, that's going to make our arrangement a little difficult." Mel's gaze darted about the room.

"Tell me about it. I have to live with the thing between my legs," he deadpanned.

She blushed and sputtered. He'd seen many sides of her, but this shy side? It was downright adorable.

"Do you always have to be so crude?" she asked, although there was more exasperation than bite in her voice.

"No, but you bring it out in me."

"Still, you can't be saying shit like that when we have a hands off policy. Unless…"

"Unless what?"

"Unless you want to change the ground rules."

"I'm listening," he said. Oh, yes. He was all ears.

"It's just, I think we can alter the rules is all." She glanced at the floor. "I know we're working together, but it isn't long term. So I'd personally like to enjoy the time we have left."

"And you'd like to enjoy me?"

He'd seen her angry and cheerful, turned on and reticent. But this little hint of vulnerability, followed up by that mischievous grin he'd come to adore—how the hell was he supposed to defend himself against *that.*

"Melody?"

She glanced at her watch, a sparkle in her eyes. "Sorry, tough guy, you're just going to have to wait for an answer to that question. I was serious. We do have important music business. We're checking out the venue for your party and we have to be there"—she checked her watch again—"in like thirty minutes. So get your naked butt up and get ready. And bring your guitar."

So, feeling something up against your leg or in your hand, and then seeing it in daylight? Two totally different things. She really didn't even fathom that he might be naked under the sheets. Stupid, because it totally made sense that he'd sleep nude. The guy liked his freedom.

But shoot, she had to pull herself together. Despite the way Aaron was blowing this off, the venue for his party was a huge deal. She knew this. The location, the lighting, the music, even the scent, could make or break an event. And this was so important for Aaron. He needed to look the part, act the part, *be* the new and improved Country Superstar Aaron Major. Classy and in control, reformed outlaw, available bachelor (*grrrr*), smart and sexy Aaron Major. All the men should want to be him and all the women should want him in their beds (double *grrrr*).

Though it wasn't a public event, the invite list included some of the biggest country music bloggers, label heads, new artists, song writers, and producers. They'd start with the influencers and work their way down. Key portions of the event would be live-streaming for fans. It couldn't be stated strongly enough how big of a deal this was.

So she had to be on her game. She could *not* be thinking about what she saw this morning—no matter how impressive it was. Her legs involuntarily squeezed together at the thought.

She rested her hand on his arm as they entered the old tavern called Pray.

"Ready to go to church?" she asked.

"I'm ready to do whatever you need me to do, Melody Sharp. You're in control today, so lead on." He held the door for her, and she gave him the hairy eyeball. Where was this coming from? She was prepared for cranky, irritable Aaron, not Mr. Accommodating. She'd have to keep on her toes today because he was surely up to something.

They walked in and Mel immediately fell in love with the space. The building had, in fact, actually been a church, but the congregation had grown so much that the pastor commissioned another building a few blocks away. She'd been told that, as a music man himself, the pastor and his choir played at the venue regularly. She thought Aaron would appreciate that.

The contractor for the remodel had done amazing work. He'd left the ceiling open, with the beams exposed, and at the back of the sanctuary had built a long, distressed wood bar made up of reclaimed lumber. The original pews were used for seating throughout the space.

The stained glass made for great lighting. Even at night, the streetlights would shine in, and if they kept the overhead lights just a little dim, it'd be perfect. Everyone would look great. Not that it was a worry with Aaron. He always looked amazing.

She couldn't help but admire him as he walked through the room, his head tipped toward the ceiling. He made her tingle all over. It unnerved her, maybe because she knew he was more than considering her idea of breaking some rules.

In the interim between her 'deal' with Miranda and see-ing Aaron sign on the dotted line, two things had crystalized in her mind: one, she would make sure that he reclaimed his fame; two, she would find a way to change some key points in their cohabitation arrangement. She wanted to make the most of every second she had left with him so when she trot-ted back home for the festival, she'd have the skills to show Teddy a thing or two. *If* she decided to meet him…and that was still a big if.

Strange. The entire reason she had started this was to teach Teddy a lesson, and yet she'd been so wrapped up in Aaron and the campaign, she'd almost forgotten about it.

The countdown had already commenced, and not only for the Last Hurrah. Aaron's days were also limited. His launch was less than two weeks away. So, she wouldn't let a moment pass without honoring what she'd set out to do when she first arrived in Atlanta. She'd have fun. Be a little wild. Discover what made *her* happy.

And Aaron Major *definitely* made her happy.

Two times with him wasn't nearly enough. She wanted all of him. As soon as possible. And she didn't feel even re-motely guilty about it. They were both having fun, doing each other huge favors, and he wasn't really a client in the traditional sense. She'd brought him to Miranda. They'd be-come friends, and really, who cared if they crossed the line every now and then in their short time together? It wasn't a conflict of interest job-wise, because she didn't plan to stay at Elite.

"So," she followed in the steps behind Aaron, "what do you think?"

"This ain't Nashville, that's for sure."

"But that's what we want, right?" She assessed the room through his eyes, looking for the best place for the stage, imagining what the room would look like from his vantage point.

"Do you think it's a little sacrilegious? You know, turning a place of worship into a bar?"

"It's just a building, Aaron. And obviously the congregation doesn't have a problem with it. The pastor brings his choir here, for crying out loud."

"With the baby Jesus hanging in the window?"

"It was a place to help people find their way. I think listening to music can help people do that as well."

"You have an answer for everything, don't you?"

"Not everything," she said. "But look, we have a bunch of places on the list. We don't have to stop here."

"But I do want to stop here. Something about this place hits me. I like it. I like it a lot. And it's symbolic. It's perfect, actually."

He began tuning his guitar, humming. The acoustics were incredible. Of course, the owner had said they were, but she had Aaron bring his guitar just to be sure. The owner was right.

This was their first stop, but she knew they wouldn't need to go any further.

Aaron took a seat on a barstool, and then his sweet music rang throughout the room, seeming to roll around, seeping into the wood.

"Play the new one that kept you up all last night." She wasn't above begging. "Will you?" Or whining.

He looked hesitant, but then nodded. "You are the only person to hear this, Mel, so don't judge me too harshly."

"What's it called?" she asked.

"'More than a Trophy.'"

A lump formed in her throat, and she couldn't say a thing. It was what she'd told him that first night she stayed with him. It was what she always wanted to be to someone. More.

Chapter Fourteen

"Don't worry, honey. It's just a song that's all," he said, tuning his guitar so he didn't have to see her face. "Inspiration comes from many places, so don't freak out. I'm not going to ask you to be my baby mama or anything."

Even as the words left his mouth, he knew he'd gone and fucked it up. Once he did catch her in his peripheral vision, Mel looked like she was damn near ready to bolt. Rigid body, flushed face, wild eyes. Tempting as hell, but that was beside the point.

Why did he have to tell her the name of the song? It just as easily could've been about anyone else. She didn't have to know. But that was him, laying it all on the table. Whether people were ready for it or not.

And from Mel's guarded expression, she was most definitely in the *not* camp.

"Let's hear it then." She smiled, but the wariness on her face hadn't yet faded.

He shifted on the stool in front of her and closed his eyes before strumming that first cord. He loved that, the quiet moment before the music. The anticipation of a song or note or a tone of a voice—it was tangible. He'd delay as long as he could…

His instrument was slung low, where it felt like home. When he first started playing, he tried riding it high like Johnny Cash—pointing it out toward the crowd like it was a gun. It was the coolest thing he ever watched a musician do. Never worked for him, though. Aaron's style was too relaxed.

But once he started playing, there was nothing slow or easy about the way he made music. The softest note was intense. And when the room filled with music, the tension radiating off Mel wasn't an issue anymore. She settled into her chair and let the song wash over her. She looked peaceful, moved even. Damn, he knew the feeling.

The lyrics were about taking risks and second chances and the beauty of finding what you need in unexpected places. He sang about a beautiful woman. About touching her. Tasting her. Giving *to* her, and taking *from* her.

Mel swayed, her eyes fixed on him.

It was almost too much, singing to her. Singing about how he wanted her. And he did. The only way to get through it was to close his eyes and lose himself in the music.

This song was like nothing he'd ever written. Sure, he'd been vulnerable before, but more in a raw, exposed way. This had a deeper feel to it, more baring emotions closer to the soul. Jesus, this was why musicians drank. Who wanted to live on the edge all the time?

When it was finally over, he opened his eyes to catch

Mel wiping a tear.

They sat there a moment in silence, and he let her recover.

"That bad, huh?" he joked, even though he had to fight through the lump in his throat to force the words out.

She stood and walked to him, slowly and deliberately.

"It was the most beautiful thing I've ever heard." Her eyes were soft, searching.

"Not bad for one of the first ones on my own." He again tried to lighten the mood, because, fuck, she was killing him right now.

"Aaron." She gave him a little punch to the shoulder. "You are so going to get laid with this song."

"Really?"

"Totally. Play that for any woman and she'll be putty in your hands."

"And what about the woman who inspired the song?" It was time. No, it wasn't convenient, but he wasn't waiting another second. She made a good point about enjoying the time she had left, and he wanted to help her do just that. They could do this, a fun fling until the launch. Hell, it might even help them both focus.

Mel's eyelids were heavy, and her breath kicked up. She wanted it, too. He could feel the heat radiating from under that proper little dress. He wanted to mess her up. He wanted to mess her up good.

"She's a little mushy," she told him. "I'll give you that."

"I like my women mushy." He took the phone that was permanently glued to her hand and looked at the clock. "Let's see how much time we have left."

"Not enough." Her voice was so raspy, so sexy, he couldn't take it any longer.

"Maybe not as much as I want, but we can work with it."
He set his guitar on the bar and pulled Mel between his legs.

"Aaron." She placed a hand on his chest in. "We can't.
Not here."

"We can, and we should." He ignored her protest, placing
his hands on her thighs while his lips dipped to her neck.
Fuck, he loved her taste, loved how she shivered when he
touched her. It was inevitable that this was going to happen.
There was a part of him that didn't want it to be here, with
such little time and privacy. He wanted to savor, not hurry.
Yet it was right in some strange way. A church, a place of
music. It was fucking beautiful, actually.

Her head turned toward him, and he used the opportunity to take those lips, capturing them with his own, nipping
and then soothing with this tongue. She opened for him,
driving him mad. He squeezed her legs before letting his
hands continue upward. Her skin was so hot it made it impossible to think clearly. And when he grazed her hip bones
with his thumbs, the ache behind his fly became unbearable.

He couldn't decide which he liked more, claiming her
with his mouth or possessing her with his hands. He was
grateful he didn't have to choose. Their tongues swirled in
a dance that was part soft and sweet, part dirty as hell. He
sucked on her tongue and she arched her back, swaying
against him. Her legs quaked.

He bypassed her sweet spot and bunched her dress
around her waist before lifting her off her toes.

They stayed there for a moment, his cock perfectly
aligned with her center and his head flooded with her seduc-
tive scent. He wanted inside. He wanted her. Like yesterday.

"Wrap your legs around me, honey," he forced out

between breaths.

She obliged, locking those long limbs around his waist. She was taut and willowy, but feather light. He clasped one hand around the base of her neck and the other just under her ass, securing her to him. She fit into his arms perfectly, just as good as his guitar. Shit, maybe even better.

He walked toward the far wall, a corner shadowed from the light that glowed through the stained glass windows. He really wanted her bathed in that light as he explored every inch of her. But they needed to be careful, just in case.

"I want you, Melody." He pushed her up against the wall, and her heavy-lidded eyes and parted lips told him everything he needed to know. He reached into his back pocket for a condom.

"So you do know where to buy these." She took the foil packet from him and opened it while he lifted her leg with one hand and unbuttoned his jeans with the other. "May I ask when?"

"The morning after the table," he managed, as the final button gave and he released himself. It was pure relief. Mel returned the condom and he sheathed his aching length in record time, before sliding her panties to the side. He needed her now, and with his cock free from its denim cell, he nestled in Mel's warmth like a kinky sort of heaven.

"Aaron," she said, leaning back into him. "I want you, too. Please don't stop."

That wouldn't be an issue.

He used the tip of his length to push against her entrance. She was drenched with her arousal and almost made him come on contact. Instead, he tightened his jaw, focused, and lifted her up, cradling her thighs. He needed her closer.

It had been a long while since he'd had sex. After his crash and burn on the music scene, he was celibate for almost two years. Not an easy way to live after having what he wanted and who he wanted whenever he wanted. Staying away from pussy was the worst kind of detox. But it allowed him to focus, to get his head right.

Since then, he'd been with women, sure. Quick hookups. Not sleazy, but nothing intense or emotional either. This, with Mel, was something new. And he wanted to make it last as long as possible. They tried fighting the attraction, the goddamn chemical reaction, but he thought it might have occurred to both of them to wonder why. At least it did with him.

They were adults, and they'd been honest with each other. And maybe most importantly, they had an expiration date. Nobody was going to get hurt.

He could feel her tightening, clenching down on the head of his cock, and it was the most exquisite sensation he'd felt in his entire life. "God, I want to be inside you."

Mel inhaled and her body shook. Yes, she wanted this as much as he did. She gave a brisk nod of her head and tightened her grip on his shoulders.

"You sure, honey?"

She clung to him and power surged through his veins in a rush. "Yes."

Using the wall for leverage, he broke away to readjust his hold on Mel. She weighed next to nothing, but he needed one free hand to get her ready. That's when he noticed the surveillance camera to their left. Shit! He'd been so lost in the moment, he didn't even think about cameras. He took inventory of their compromising position. Thankfully, he was completely covering Mel, so she was safe. And the corner was so dark there was no way the camera would be able to pick up anything. He did a quick study of the room. Cameras were angled at the cash registers and toward the entrance, another on the dance floor. Seeing as how Mel had been given keys to come into Pray, and how no one else was in the building, he doubted they'd even have the security cameras running. Still, to be sure, he shifted her deeper into the corner.

She went up on her toes, one leg slinging around his waist, her hips pressing against his. Yeah, she was one hundred percent right there with him.

And hell if he could wait another second. He tucked his hand between them and grazed a single finger through her folds, into a pool of slick heat. He couldn't help the hiss that slipped through his clenched jaw. He didn't expect her to be so wet, so ready. The world began to blur a little just then, and he damn near dropped her. God, he wanted to do this with more finesse, more time. But they didn't have it. With a knuckle, he eased her open further while his thumb stroked her clit. Her legs wrapped around him like a vice, and he relished the fact that he was the man between her legs. There was no other place he'd rather be.

He positioned the tip of his cock against her entrance, circling her in preparation. And yes, maybe teasing her a bit. She deserved it for the state she put him in, and he wanted her distracted when he pushed inside, because he wasn't sure how gentle he could be. Her nails dug in his shoulders and it was the best kind of pain.

But just as he was ready to fill her, the door rattled. The damn fucking heavy-ass door.

"Melody." A squeaky voice rang out and bounced across the room.

"Motherfucker," he hissed, quickly sliding her down his body and smoothing her dress in the process. She gave him a look that asked, "Am I good?"

He nodded and faced the wall, tucking his length back into his pants.

"Right here," Mel called out, walking into the light. "We were admiring the wooden beams."

One in particular.

Jesus, his pants formed a perfect tent, and *it* showed no signs of going down. But when the manager of the bar cackled at something Mel had said, it was a welcome bucket of ice water. That woman's voice was about the ugliest sound he'd ever heard. Lucky for him.

Still, this need wasn't going away anytime soon.

So he made his plans.

Chapter Fifteen

Yes, it was true what they say about musicians and their hands, Mel thought as they drove to the next venue. Who *they* were and what *they* said, she wasn't exactly sure. Point was, the cowboy had moves.

"But I thought we both loved the space at Pray," Aaron said on the ride to a place called The Lowdown.

"We do," she said. "Now it's just a matter of due diligence. We can't seem too eager. And you never know... what if something better comes along?"

"I'm a guy of instinct," he said. "I don't believe in waiting around. If it's right, you know it. What about you?"

She'd just have to sidestep that one. In her sexually frustrated haze, she wasn't up to answering the big questions. "Um, either way, we have a budget to work with, and if we know what others are offering, it puts us in a better position for negotiation." She sang the last word and prepared for the ribbing. It never came. Instead he sat there with the strangest expression. Color her happy, because it just might have been a look that said he was impressed.

"We're here," she said pulling up in front of a nondescript corporate building with a neon sign. She glanced over at Aaron and he looked like he ate some expired yogurt. She had in fact witnessed that very expression the other day in the kitchen. "And be good."

"Welcome, y'all." A stocky man with a full beard greeted them at the entrance. The inside was no better. It was a boring, cookie-cutter space that was plain wrong for what they were trying to do. They didn't let on, and Mel went forward with negotiations. Aaron later told her it was a waste of time, but she knew it'd pay off.

They made their way through the city's biggest hotspots, and by the end of the day, it was unanimous: they didn't like the Lowdown, or the Fixture, or Big Daddy's. Aaron was right. When you know, you know.

Mel wasn't wrong, either, and when she called Pray with all her new intel, she negotiated a hell of a deal.

She emailed Rita photos and information, hoping that keeping her in the loop would make her easier to deal with. The woman was territorial, and she didn't like another woman on her turf. Shit, if she knew the two of them had been shacking up, it wouldn't be pretty.

They walked back to the car and Aaron looked edible in his jeans and T-shirt with the guitar hanging off his back and the Atlanta skyline in the distance. She took a quick photo of him.

"What's all this about? You've been snapping pictures all day. Just what are you using all of these for?" He wiggled his brows. "Come on, you can tell me."

"For your Twitter account." She made some quick edits to the picture and sent it over to Tiffany, who was managing his social media sites.

"Oh no, Mel." He growled at her as she snapped another photo. He was pretty cute when he was mad, so she took another.

"Heh. I'll have to come up with a good caption for that one." Mel's phone rang and she ignored it. This was important. It may have seemed fun and silly, but it was all part of the bigger plan.

"I'm not into all the self-promo, narcissist crap. The party, the interviews, fine. I get that. But I don't need followers or tweeters or whatever the hell they are. I don't need anyone stroking my ego…well, other than you, honey."

"So sweet." She giggled.

"I'm serious, Mel. I have to maintain some level of privacy."

"This is part of my promo plan for your release," she assured him. "You need to get out there and let fans into your life—just a little bit. But I promise you, we will manage it. This is how people communicate in 2015, darlin'. You need to join in or be left behind."

"Well, we wouldn't want that now, would we?" Sarcasm, like everything else, was a good look on him. So she flashed her camera once again.

"Must be nice always making your own rules." The city street began filling up with the evening commuters. They'd spent the entire workday downtown searching for the perfect place, but to Mel it didn't seem nearly that long.

"Hey, just like you, I've got bills to pay." He placed his hand on the small of her back, guiding her through the crowded streets.

"About that," she said. "I've been watching you, and you are a simple man. No flashy possessions. No drug or hooker problem that I've noticed so far. So what is it that you spend your money on?"

"My brother." He didn't elaborate, and that made Mel a little sad. She thought they were beyond that point.

"So he's the one into drugs and hos?" she quipped, trying to lighten the suddenly intense mood. "You tell him I said he needs to quit ASAP."

"I'll tell him you said so." He grinned, but it never fully reached his eyes. "I also help him with school and some other things."

He didn't seem to want to share the "other things," so Mel let it go. When they finally reached her car, her phone started going off again. She'd take care of it when she got home. It could wait.

"You're really good at this, you know?" Aaron said, opening the car door for her.

"Yep. Making things pretty. It's what I do."

"It's a helluva lot more than that," he said. "You know I hate it, but I do see how hard you work, and I get that there's a high level of strategy involved. What I don't get is how you got into trouble with Miranda in the first place. Why you're not killing it. Honey, you're a natural at this."

"Maybe I've never taken it that seriously before. It's different working with you." She left it at that, because there were some things she wanted to keep to herself, too.

It was the longest day of his life, especially everything that came after the visit to Pray. He didn't see why it was necessary to tour all the other places, anyway. Okay, other than the bill. Mel saved him a ton of money. He wasn't joking when he said she was good at her job. Though he may have rather paid the asking price so they could've finished what they'd started at the first bar, but it was like she flipped the switch to business and was no longer interested. It was abrupt, and harsh, and so not like Mel.

He'd become a lovesick schoolboy, and it was damn pathetic, but at that particular moment he didn't care if the launch of the album was a complete bust. Mel consumed him. And he let her know it each chance he got. A touch on her hand. His breath on her neck. The press of his body close to hers. Damn right he was going to torture her. Especially when she gave him the cold shoulder.

There was so much tension, or sexual energy, in the car, he wasn't sure either one of them would survive the drive home. He wished he'd agreed to let her take the wheel so he could continue his punishment. But in some ways, he was still a caveman. He was the driver, not the passenger. Always.

Though once he pulled up into the drive of the apartment and put the car in park, he wasted no time. His head descended toward her, and he nibbled on that sweet spot below her ear. She didn't seem to notice as she typed away on her phone, which was completely unlike her. That didn't sit well with him. At. All.

Had she had her fill of him already? Gotten what she needed from him with this gig and ready to move on?

"All right." He took her phone. "What is going on? You're making me feel like an asshole right now."

"Give it back." She didn't meet his eye, she just batted around for the phone. He flipped it over to see what was so goddamn important. "Stop." She batted some more. "Don't read that. Give it back."

Once he read the screen, he wished he had listened to her.

He read it again then handed the cell back to her.

"It's nothing," she said, turning the phone off. "He's an idiot. It doesn't matter."

Too bad it mattered to him. A lot. It was a post on that shitty Twitter feed he didn't want to get involved with in the first place. The first post said he was a hack and he should've stayed out of the public eye. The second commented that Jayden was the only real talent in their band. There was a bunch more, but he couldn't read them all on the small screen.

"This is all part of it," Mel said. "Your intro into the world of trolls. But there are more good people out there, I promise you. And once we start posting music clips, you are going to explode on social media. It sucks now, but you have to trust me."

Trusting Mel wasn't the issue. The issue was, what if those trolls were right?

As they walked up the stairs, Mel took his hand as if it was the most natural thing in the world. And somehow it helped. He hated and loved her effect on him, all at the same time, and was starting to worry how he'd be able to do all this once she went back home. The thought made his chest ache.

But when he reached the landing, he snapped his hand away instantly. Once he noticed that the door to his apartment was cracked open, his instincts took over.

A loud rattling came from inside.

Shit.

He quickly pushed Mel behind him. The door was closed when they'd left, but he couldn't remember who was the last person out, or if it had been locked.

He took a step inside and snagged one of the guitars that was leaning up against the wall. He held it like a bat, readying to strike.

The sound of slamming cabinets coming from the kitchen had him raising the instrument and charging inside. He rounded the corner, adrenaline kicking as he saw the large man at his counter. His back was toward him, so Aaron at least had the element of surprise.

But when the man turned around, all the air left his chest.

"Jesus Christ, you fucking idiot." He lowered the guitar. "What are you doing here?"

It was Jayden. In his kitchen, with a goddamn bowl of Frosted Flakes.

"Rita sent me," he said as he shoved a bite in his mouth. "Like I could stay away with your new single ready to drop and all the shit they're saying about you online. We need to make this album killer, dude." Milk dribbled off his chin, and Aaron was ready to beat him down. The fucker almost caused a heart attack.

"Ever hear of a phone call to text or warn me?" Or did Rita? All he knew was that she would be long gone after the single dropped. He didn't know what bothered him more, that Rita was overstepping boundaries again, or that she didn't trust he could do the album without Jay's help.

"Why would I call?" Jayden asked. "I never have before."

"Dude, we're in a major city, not some country-ass town. You can't come in here unannounced. I could've seriously hurt you. I thought you were robbing the place."

Jayden waved him off. "Well then, maybe you shouldn't leave your door open, dumb-ass. And what were you going to do if I was a thief? Play me to sleep?"

"No, I was going to smash your face in."

Mel rounded the corner and Jayden's eyes proceeded to pop out of his head, much like Aaron's did the first time he got a look at her.

"I'm sorry," Mel said into her cell. "False alarm."

"You called the cops?" Aaron asked her.

"Yes, but I take it you know this intruder?" She sized up his lead guitar player and co-writer. He didn't like that one bit. The ladies fucking loved Jayden Jones. He had that all-American boy look—sandy hair, blue eyes, and a body he spent hours at the gym creating.

"This is Jayden," he told her.

"Oh." She moved a little too quickly to shake his ex-partner's hand. "I've heard a lot about you."

"Really?" Jayden said. "Because I'm a little in the dark over here. Who might you be?"

Mel blushed, and shifted her weight uncomfortably.

"That's because I haven't talked to you in weeks," Aaron said by way of explanation. "Mel is my publicist, our pub-licist, really…and my *roommate*." He cringed saying the last word, and looked at Mel's response. She was impassive. Surely, she didn't want him explaining their relationship to him, right? Did she even think of it—of him—that way?

Forget the hand basket—this day was going to hell in a

freaking wheelbarrow.

"Isn't that convenient," Jay said in response, a shit-eating grin stretching across his face.

"Yeah," Mel added. "Just a temporary situation. I needed a place to crash and Aaron was kind enough to let me stay."

He'd never seen her so flustered before. He wasn't sure what to make of it. The whole damn day had been a rollercoaster of emotion and now, fuck, he had to deal with Jayden.

"So let's hear it then," Jayden said, not one for small talk. A trait he usually found appealing.

Mel made herself scarce while the two of them went and made music.

She worked from the spare bedroom for a few hours, trying not to listen as they played. She thought the song was perfect, but Jayden had plenty to say about it. Speaking of, she had to check in with Tiffany about the Twitter fiasco.

"Hi Mel." She answered on the first ring. "You're not going to believe this."

"Good or bad?" Mel held her breath.

"Good," Tiff squealed. "So good."

Mel stretched out on the bed. "Okay, lay it on me."

"So, as you know, we opened the account yesterday morning and there was a slow, but steady, rise all day as we posted about his launch. In the first twenty-four hours, he had twenty-five thousand followers."

"Not bad." She agreed, though she wanted more.

"But then you started sending me the photos today, and all of those clever tweets, and it started to rise. Big time. The haters started chiming in, which you expected. So I posted the videos you sent over, and it got insane out there."

"Verdict?" Mel asked. She had planned this entire campaign out, step by step. Now she'd see if it paid off.

"Tonight we're at five-hundred thousand followers, and all of Aaron's former fans are really active. I'm getting all the new fan pages up and that's gaining speed as well."

"Ohmygod." Now it was Mel squealing.

Aaron came rushing in. "What happened?" He gripped her by the arms, a worried looked washed across his face. "Are you okay?"

Mel nodded and thanked Tiff for all of her hard work before hanging up. "This is huge, baby."

"What is?" he asked. "Tell me now because you scared the shit out of me. Two times in one night is too much."

"I'm sorry." She pulled him down on the bed next to her. "But look at this," she pulled up his account, "you have a half million followers in just two days, Aaron."

"And that's a lot, right?"

"A helluva lot. This is great. There is major buzz about you and your launch. If all goes well, we will see quantifiable sales from the social media campaign. I don't want to jinx it, but you are going to be a star again."

"I don't need to be a star." He took her hands and kissed each finger. "But some sales sure would be nice."

"It's happening for you Aaron. I can feel it. So go out there and finish up that album."

"Yes, ma'am." He saluted before walking out the door.

Mel was on a cloud as she ticked off every single one of her to-do items. The guys were still going at it, and though she tried not to eavesdrop, she couldn't help it, so she cracked her door open to hear what was going on.

"No," Jayden said, soft and low. "Stripped down. A lot of space. Like this." He played the chorus and hummed along, "let the lyrics do it for this one, and we'll do a bluesy sound behind it."

"Yeah," Aaron said, before belting out the words. "That's it."

She heard the beer cans crack open after he finished. "Hey, Melody," Jayden called. "Get your sweet behind out here so we have someone to play to."

He didn't have to ask her twice, though he could refrain from talking about her *sweet behind*, thank you very much.

Aaron sounded great but looked a little foggy. Unease prickled in her belly. She looked around the room and counted the beer cans scattered about, and noted the half-empty tequila bottle that wasn't in the apartment before Jayden arrived, quickly figuring out the reason for Aaron's dreamy demeanor.

This might be part of the *process*, but it made her jittery. And she couldn't say a thing. It wasn't her place. So if she couldn't beat them, she guessed she'd join them.

After several more beers and the rest of the tequila bottle, they were all feeling pretty comfortable, and Mel forgot all about her jitters.

Aaron and Jayden shared stories about the old days, of growing up together and the first days in the band. It was the first chance Mel really caught a glimpse of who Aaron was before he came to Atlanta, who he was outside of the bubble they'd been living in for the last week.

Though, on several occasions, when Jayden was reminiscing aloud, Aaron would level a look on him that said 'go any further and you're going to lose a testicle.' Part of her was thankful, the other part was curious.

Maybe if she heard what really happened when they were traveling the country, she'd heed her brain's warning, the one that'd been telling her to end the physical part of their relationship before she got hurt. Trouble was, whenever Aaron was around, it was her body making all of the decisions.

A phone rang from the other room and Aaron wiped a hand over his face. "Shit, I was supposed to call Rita when we got back today. You two entertain yourselves for minute, this shouldn't take too long."

When he left, Jayden got up from the stool he'd brought in from kitchen and plopped down next to her on the couch.

She was buzzed, but it didn't stop her from noticing that something wasn't quite right with Jayden. The way his eyes darted around the room, unable to focus, set warning bells off in her head.

"So Melody," he said, draping an arm over her shoulder. "How'd you get to be so chummy with my boy?"

She didn't like his tone, so she kept her answer vague and guarded. "I used to live around here."

"You did?" he said, squeezing her a little closer, letting his eyes rake over her body. He was way too close, and her body finally listened to her brain as she pulled away from him.

But he anticipated her move and tightened his grip. "So are you ready for us," he said in her ear, before his hands snaked around her waist.

A strangled scream ripped from her throat, and in the next instant, Aaron dove at him like a linebacker, breaking the glass on the coffee table. In seconds, he had Jayden up against the wall, his hand fisted in his shirt.

"Get the fuck off her," he yelled. Jayden was dumbfounded. Drunk. Stoned. Stupid.

"Sorry," he said, making no move to fight him. "I thought…"

She waited for an explanation that didn't come.

"It ain't like that," Aaron spit out, and Mel thought she might be sick. They'd done this before? Shared a woman?

His words that day she asked him about his past came to her now. *Rock and Roll has nothing on the crazy shit that goes on in Country. You have no idea.*

She sure did now.

"I'm sorry," Jay said over and over in his drunken stupor.

"Sleep it off, man," Aaron said. "Take the spare bedroom and sleep it off."

Now, wait a minute.

"You're staying with me," Aaron said, reaching for her hand, not giving her any choice in the matter. "I'm not letting you out of my sight."

He didn't say a word as he led her to his room, but she wasn't going to let this go.

"Are you going to tell me what that shit was all about?" she asked, taking a seat on his bed.

"I'd rather not," he said, helping her remove her shoes.

"Well, are into that? Were you expecting me to go along with it?"

"Fuck, no," he said, stroking her legs now. "I told you what it was like before. Mel, I wasn't myself back then, and I have no intention of going back to that, ever."

Mel knew she should be mad at him, disgusted even.

Who does that shit? And what kind of world did he live in? And worse, could she believe him? Her mind was foggy, her thoughts scattered. She needed sleep.

"Let's talk about it in the morning, okay?" Aaron pulled the covers down while Mel slipped off her clothes, leaving her tank and panties on. He followed her into the bed, his arm wrapped around her stomach, and he pulled her close.

She let him.

For now...

Chapter Sixteen

Aaron woke in a panic when he felt for Mel in his bed and she wasn't there. His mind went to the worst case scenario—which he realized would be her leaving, especially after everything that had happened that night, and how shitty she must've felt after the way Jayden treated her—as if she weren't doing a real, worthwhile job for him and was only there for his entertainment. She had been so disrespected, and that was the last thing he wanted her to feel after she'd done so much for him. He respected her more than she'd ever know.

If Jayden ruined this for him, he'd kill the bastard.

He jolted up and took inventory of the apartment. No sign of her in his bedroom—her belongings were all gone. Even her smell had faded. Hallway—same thing. He moved to the door to the spare bedroom and stood outside of it, too chickenshit to turn the knob. He couldn't bear to see it empty.

"Mel," he called out instead. "Melody." He swallowed the lump lodged in his throat.

"In here," she said and he almost broke down.

He followed her voice into the kitchen, and there she was, set up at the table, as she had been for the past few weeks.

"I thought you left," he said, taking a seat across from her. She had dark circles under her eyes and looked absolutely worn out, and it made him feel like hell.

"I wouldn't do that," she said. "We had a deal."

"I'm not going to hold you to it after what you had to put up with last night. But can we talk about it?"

"No," she blurted. "Not now. I think it would be best to go back to our original business deal, to keep our relationship professional and honor your rules. Remember? No complications."

Right. If only she knew, she'd never be a complication to him.

D ays passed and they never did talk about it. He couldn't bring himself to. To have his past collide with his present in that way, in front of *her*, was more than he could take. After Jayden left, Mel moved back into the spare bedroom. It was hell. He wanted her in his bed, but how could he ask after she witnessed the ugliness that had been his life?

She didn't hold it against him though. She was sweet and professional and her pleasant self. But he didn't want pleasant. He wanted her cursing and laughing and moving under him screaming his name.

Not very likely.

"Let's try it again," Mel said as they practiced his act for the launch party.

She was pestering him about the way he was playing, the look on his face, the tone of his voice, and he was about ready to lose it.

"I've got it," he told her. "The single is already cut. I think I know how to sing the goddamn song, Mel."

"Yeah, you cut it in a studio without an audience. You had the privacy you love and you could scowl all you want."

Why couldn't she just leave him the hell alone?

"Why should this be different?" he challenged. "This song is about a freaking nightmare." Most of the album was dark, raw, and gritty.

"It is, and it's so emotional. So incredible. Let us feel that with you. If you're going to do this, darlin', you have to do it all the way. You have to be an entertainer."

He groaned, not looking at her, picking at his guitar. He didn't have his band up there with him, which was part of the problem, but he wasn't about to haul them over to Atlanta for a dress rehearsal. And he definitely wasn't ready to see Jayden yet. Not after last night's fiasco.

So he dug deep, and when she said, "Play for me," he did just that.

His eyes didn't leave hers the entire time.

It wasn't perfect, but he was getting there.

Chapter Seventeen

"**D**id you know Margaret Mitchell only wrote one book in her entire life," Mel told Aaron once he stumbled into the kitchen and downed a cup of coffee. She let him ease into the day until she couldn't take it any longer. She'd been up since six a.m., setting up an official campaign headquarters at the kitchen table, and she had big plans for the day.

Poor Aaron had been up late again working on a song, which was something she hoped to address. If he was receptive.

He was still a little ornery from the way she'd pestered him during yesterday's session, and exhausted from trying to finish his album. She wanted to cheer him up and, truth be told, kick him in the ass a little. Since he'd walked into her life, he'd inspired her to go after what she wanted and do things she never thought she could.

It was time to return the favor.

Aaron now had four songs for the album, but he only seemed happy with one of them. In her mind, it was totally okay for him to feel that way. Though she was over the moon for the song she inspired, there was no denying his single was off the charts amazing.

"Who the hell is Margaret Mitchell?" He finally responded, as he checked out the large calendar on the table and picked up the rainbow of sticky notes sitting next to it. He began peeling them off one by one.

"Oh, don't tell me," she said, painfully disappointed. "You're a writer, how can you not know the author of *Gone with the Wind*?"

"I'm a songwriter." He mimed playing the guitar. "And I'm using the term loosely. But you're right, that is a little embarrassing, especially when we're in Atlanta and all. Isn't this where she wrote the book?"

She could feel her eyes growing wide. *He knew that?*

"Impressive, cowboy. Yes, this is where she wrote the book."

"Didn't she win the Pulitzer or something?" he said in a yawn. Poor guy, she definitely needed to help him fix this.

"Honey, now you're starting to redeem yourself."

"I really hope you mean that," he said softly. His eyes warmed in a way that she liked to think was only for her.

She knew his response wasn't about the game of trivia they had going on. It was about what had happened when Jayden was in town. And maybe, deep down, that's what she was talking about, too. He'd handled the situation with Jayden the best way he could, and it hardly seemed fair to hold him accountable for his band mate's action. He'd told her many times about how out of control his lifestyle used to be. It wasn't like he was trying to hold anything back from her.

She pulled the sticky notes away from his nervous hands, placing a bright green one on his nose. It was best to keep things light for now, so she continued with her story. "So Margaret Mitchell, Atlanta native, as you know, wrote one of the most beloved novels of all time, and never wrote another. She'd been a journalist and wrote hundreds of newspaper articles, and some others things as well, but never another novel."

"Why not?" He leaned against the table now, getting into the story. The way he listened to her always made her feel important. Smart even. Like she had something worthwhile to say. Or maybe it was that she felt so comfortable around him that she said worthwhile things. Either way, he lifted her up.

"Well," she went on. "Margaret was hit by a car on Peachtree Street and died, but it was many years later. Who knows? Maybe she only had that one book in her."

"Jesus, Mel." His words were harsh, but he was smirking now. "I was getting ready for some nice uplifting story and you smack me in the face with death. And hey, isn't your office building on Peachtree Street?"

"Yeah, but it's not the same one. Didn't you know half the streets in this city are named Peachtree?"

"I didn't." He pinched the bridge of his nose. "Why are you telling me this, anyway?"

"Because sometimes one is all you need." She took his hand then, unable to stop herself. How she missed those capable hands. "Maybe your single is the one big story you have, and maybe you'll continue to write things that people enjoy but you'll never reach the level of satisfaction you did with that one. That's okay. If writing doesn't feel good to you, get a new songwriter to help, or get some of the guys from the band back together. Hell, work it out with Jayden if you need to. But stop killing yourself over this."

"You'd be comfortable if I worked with Jayden again?" He tightened his grip on her hand.

"Yes," she said, feeling the weight of the last few days lift. "Don't get me wrong, I don't want to be around when you do. But this is your career we're talking about."

"And you don't think I'd be giving up if I worked with some other people on this?"

"God no, Aaron. You proved you can write; you don't have to do it all on your own. Who does that, anyway?"

"I thought it'd be the only way to stay in control," he admitted, finally getting to the real issue.

"Maybe the only way to stay in control is to share the burden so you don't burn yourself out. And don't take this the wrong way, but those rules you first told me about—no band, no relationships, nothing on the scene in Nashville? I think your rules suck."

"Hey now," he released her hand and pointed a finger in her direction. "Those are fighting words."

"I'm serious," she said. "I think they've been a crutch so you can avoid what happened. I think you need to go out and break every one of them."

"What are you saying, Mel?" Those soft eyes disappeared and a pair of guarded ones took their place. He wasn't going to like this, but...

"I think you need to go up to Nashville for a visit."

He packed his bag that night because his flight was early the next morning. He couldn't believe he was going back to Nashville after all of this time. His hands shook thinking about it, which only made him more determined.

Mel had a point. He had to stop hiding and hoping the past would fade away. Because that wasn't happening. It was up to him to change his story. Jayden and another songwriter they used to be tight with said yes when he asked if they'd work with him. They were the best and that's who he needed on this.

He tossed the bag next to his guitar by the side of his bedroom door before jumping into bed. The clock flashed 12:10.

At 2:17, he was no closer to dreamland. He wasn't the only one.

Mel padded by his door on a trip back from the bathroom and stopped when he rolled over. "Can't sleep either?" she whispered.

"Not a wink."

"Want some company?"

"More than you know." He flipped the blanket over, and Mel immediately covered her eyes. "I'm decent." He chuckled, showing her he was wearing his boxer briefs. "I didn't want to accidently shock you again, especially with everything that's happened."

"Good," she said. "That's good." Was he imagining it, or did she look a little disappointed?

She climbed in and her scent hit him instantly. This time,

though, it somehow relaxed him rather than giving him a raging hard-on. Hell, that was almost worse. Because that meant his need for her was becoming much more than physical.

And that was one problem he wasn't sure he had the strength to face.

Chapter Eighteen

Mel woke up alone in Aaron's bed and missed him immediately. Probably a good thing, because it got her up and into the office before anyone else arrived. Miranda had given her a pass to do much of the work with Aaron offsite, but the days she went into the office, she was usually the first to arrive—with the exception of Tiffany—and the last to leave.

It wasn't intentional. When she became immersed in a project, the days flew by and she hardly noticed when she was the last one in her cube. Even the Ice Queen didn't bother her as much, maybe because she usually beat her to the punch.

Until today.

"Melody," Miranda sang when she picked up the early morning call on her desk phone.

"Yes, ma'am?" She certainly hadn't missed these calls.

"My office," she snapped. "Now."

"Shit," Mel spit under her breath. This wasn't good.

"What do you need?" Tiffany was next to her in the very next second.

"Do a quick search on Aaron and his label," Mel said as she snagged her iPad, notebook and the campaign file. "Something must've happened. Miranda's summoning me."

Tiffany typed away and Mel checked her email and sent a quick text to Aaron before moving to Tiffany's cubical. "Here it is," Tiffany said, with a Nashville news website pulled up on her screen. The headline read: COUNTRY MUSIC STARS ARRESTED IN PROSTITUTION RING.

Oh no. This was not happening.

Mel quickly scanned the article because Miranda would be buzzing her again any second if she didn't hightail it to her office. It wasn't as bad as it seemed. Thankfully, she had something to work with. One, the report said police had been watching the suspects for weeks, and Aaron just landed in Nashville this morning. Two, though the article mentioned Aaron by name, it did not state whether or not he was arrested. If he wasn't, they'd spin it. Wrong place, wrong time. No charges had been filed. They'd deal with his reputation later.

"He didn't do anything," Mel told Tiffany. "Get your hands on the arrest records. Stop any promo tweets and social media alerts set to go out today. And set up a lunch with Genn Foley. She's in my computer contacts."

"What time do you want to meet her?" Tiffany asked.

"Any time the three of us are all open at the same time. I need you on this, too."

Mel raced to Miranda's office, not bothering with the three knocks. "I've got it under control," she said before taking a seat.

"Let's hear it," Miranda said.

"Aaron only arrived in Nashville this morning, to meet with some musicians to finish up his album. But the situation this morning is stemming from an ongoing investigation. Police have been on the suspects for weeks. So Aaron couldn't be involved."

Mel's phone beeped and she looked down to see a note from Tiffany: *Aaron's been released. No charges filed.*

"Why was he taken into custody, then?" Miranda pushed.

"We're getting to the bottom of that now, so I've got to go." Mel stood up before being dismissed. "Don't worry, I've got this."

She prayed that was the truth.

So yeah, Nashville once again had him by the balls. His head throbbed on the ride to the police station. Fuck, they were only allowed one call and he needed to make ten. His arrest would be all over the airwaves by now. The paparazzi were there for the entire thing. They always staked out the Nashville airport and that's where this little event all went down.

Prostitution charges, the cops said. What were the goddamn chances?

Mel would be pissed as hell about now, and Rita would be freaking out with the calls coming in from his label. And there was absolutely nothing he could do about it.

The officer led Aaron, Jayden, and their old friend Toby Lee into the station and brought them into three separate rooms. He tried to keep calm, reminding himself that he'd done nothing wrong.

Not an easy thing to do when one minute he was talking music in the passenger seat of Jayden's car, and the next he was spread eagle, leaning over the hood with a cop's hands all over him.

Inside the station, he sat at a table in a small room with no widows, desperate for his cell phone. They'd taken it from him during the mortifying frisking procedure. God dammit! He couldn't believe this was happening.

Graham would be waking up to this shit. Not that he and Jayden were big news anymore, but their buddy Toby Lee was. So it would definitely get some play.

A cop who looked like a baby—mid-twenties, tops— came in to question him.

"Mr. Major," he said, stiffly. "Do you want to tell me what happened?"

"Absolutely," Aaron said. "I flew into town today, and my buddies came to pick me up at the airport. You can easily verify my flight."

"Do you live here?"

"No," Aaron spoke slowly and clearly. He was innocent. But it didn't feel like it in his current position. "I live in Atlanta."

"Travel here often?" the officer asked, perplexed.

"This is my first time in seven years."

"Okay." The officer cocked his head. Aaron was unsure whether or not it was a good or bad thing, but apparently he said something that surprised him. "Just tell me what happened."

"I was coming into town to work with two songwriters

I know. I'm finishing up an album and I needed some help. Jayden Jones came to pick me up from the airport, the other writer, Toby Lee, was in the back with a woman I didn't know."

"Was this typical for Mr. Lee, to have women in the back of cars?"

"Like I said, I haven't been here for seven years, so I have no idea." He wasn't about to do Toby any favors—if the woman was a prostitute, and he knew about it, Aaron had no problem hanging him out to dry.

"And then?" The officer probed.

"Then nothing. That's all. They picked me up curbside, we drove out toward the freeway, and two squad cars stopped us and brought us here."

"Smith." Another man opened the door and leaned in. "A minute?"

Christ, now what? Aaron wiped his sweaty palms on his jeans and waited for what felt like hours. The clock said it was only about twenty minutes. He should probably call for an attorney. Technically, he knew he shouldn't even be talking to the police without counsel present. But attorneys said *guilty*, and he'd done nothing wrong. Man, he'd made that call so many times in the past, he just couldn't do it again.

"Mr. Major you are free to go," Officer Smith told him when he returned, and that was it. No explanation or apology.

He stopped by the desk to sign for his belongings, cringing when they handed him his phone. He turned it on and the thing lit up like Vegas, but he couldn't dial Mel's number fast enough.

"I didn't do it," he said when she picked up before the first ring finished.

"I know that," she said.

"You do?"

"Of course."

"Who'd you talk to?" He took a seat in the waiting area, unsure how much longer his legs would hold him.

"I didn't need to talk to anyone," she said, and her certainty relieved him beyond words. "Prostitution, really? I did call the police department right away, and we just heard you would not be charged. God, Aaron. I'm just so sorry I told you to go."

"What doesn't kill you, right?" His voice was shaky.

"Are you okay?"

"I will be."

"Just get home," she told him. "There's a flight in ninety minutes and there's a ticket waiting for you."

"Okay," he said, getting up to go outside. Cab to the airport. That, he could do.

As he walked out of the station, unsure where to hail a taxi, Rita entered his line of sight.

"Oh honey," she said, putting her arms around him. "Are you okay?"

"Yeah, but I need a ride."

"That's why I'm here," she said, putting a hand on his arm to lead him to her Mercedes. He hated being fussed over, but he was too mentally drained to care at this point. That was not an experience he'd like to relive.

He followed her in a fog.

"Should we go back to my place?" she asked when she pulled out of the police parking lot. "You could lie low and crash there for a few days."

"No, I just need to get home," he said.

"I don't know if that's such a good idea." She flipped on her blinker, seeming a little too upbeat about the situation. "I don't think you should be alone dealing with this shit storm."

"I'm not alone," he said without thinking. "I have Mel."

Chapter Nineteen

She had to admit, part of her was happy Aaron told Rita they were living together. Even though the situation was only temporary, Rita didn't seem to know that. She must've called her as soon as she dropped off Aaron at the airport.

Then she proceeded to give her an earful about taking advantage of her client, and accused her of being a gold digger. She also said that she'd expose her after Aaron's launch.

For some reason, Mel wasn't worried.

She knew there was something more going on with Rita than your typical business pissing contest. It was clear the woman had it bad for Aaron. But Mel couldn't be bothered with that at the moment. The more urgent matter was making Aaron all clean and sparkly again.

The music media was currently in hater mode—rehashing all of Aaron's bad boy behavior—so they needed to combat that ASAP. It was a good thing she had all of this work to do, because sitting around waiting for him to get home would've killed her, otherwise.

"Holy hell, girl," Genn said when she arrived at the Taco Shop to meet Mel and Tiffany for lunch. "I can't even keep up with all of this craziness."

Mel thought with three great minds on it, they should have a Clean-up Aaron Plan together before the bill arrived.

The three women brainstormed a dozen ideas, and Tiff had already started the social media campaign, which was simple: get the facts out there, leading with the fact that Aaron was not charged with any crime.

They were working on prong three of the plan when a miracle landed on their lap. Jayden Jones went on Good Day Nashville once he was released, and told the world what happened, completely taking responsibility, along with Toby Lee, for the events and clearing Aaron of any wrongdoing.

But it still wasn't enough. The word *prostitution* was a sticky one that would hang on for a while, so they needed more goodwill, especially where women were concerned. As part of the original plan, Mel would to set up the potential of a celebrity romance to create some buzz once the single dropped. But now she had a completely new reason for it.

Putting Aaron close to a likeable, iconic woman would be the best thing for his reputation, and Mel had the perfect candidate.

June Skye was a country goddess and all-around good girl. If she took an interest in the cowboy, well then, he must be good.

She just had to get Ms. Skye to sign off on it.

"Come here, darlin'," Aaron said as soon as she walked through the door.

She met him on the sofa, no questions asked, sliding onto his lap and sinking into his warmth. "Are you okay?" she asked, peppering his face with light kisses.

"I am now." His low voice aroused and seduced her as he took her chin in his hand to coax her closer, until his lips reached hers. He kissed her then, slow and soft at first. She didn't stop him. And when his hands trailed over her body and she leaned into him, he intensified the kiss, plunging his tongue deeper with each thrust. God, she needed this, needed him. She moaned into his mouth. She couldn't say no. She could never say no to him. But she wanted to hear more of that lazy drawl. She wanted to record it in her mind so she'd always have a small piece of him.

"Tell me what you want," she asked, willing to give him just about anything in that moment.

"I want *you*, Melody Sharp. Always."

They had gone through so much together in the past few weeks that they needed some relief. She tried not to read too much more into it. She couldn't—and that was simply self-preservation talking, because she was falling…hard.

She knew his words meant "I want you until the campaign is over," but maybe tonight she'd let herself pretend. She would take what she wanted for a change.

Aaron reached for her hand, slowly reeling her in. He was determined, in control, but he was going to give her time to decide. They had never gone all the way—geez, what was she now? A virginal co-ed?

It'd been far too long since she'd done this. But that was the way it went, right? Date three: a little finger action. Date four: oral. Date five or six: ball each other's brains out. She was sure she read that on one of those online dating sites. Of course, their progression didn't follow any of those rules.

But it felt like it was time. Oh, how she wanted it to be time.

With a strangled groan, Aaron kissed her again. Lightly at first, testing, waiting for her to open to him. She encouraged him by parting her lips and molding her body to his. She couldn't help but notice exactly how ready he was for her. And in the next moment, his hands were everywhere—touching and tugging, reducing her to an aching mess of need.

"Did I ever tell you how much I fucking adore these little dresses of yours?"

"Mmm." She tried to focus on his question. "I believe you did tell me that at Pray."

"That's right, I did. But I'm sorry, sugar. This time it needs to go. I want to see all of you." He pulled the dress over her head, leaving her in nothing but her skivvies once again. "Damn, I've wanted to do this ever since we were interrupted there."

"So have I," she gasped, as he took her mouth. Then, before she could sense what happened, Aaron stood up and skillfully worked off his own jeans in the process. He pushed up against her, and even with the thin layer of cotton between them, it felt better than…anything.

He stripped her of her bra and cupped her breasts, gliding his thumbs over her nipples. She arched her back, leaning into his touch. Then in a not-so-smooth motion, they both freed themselves of their underwear in record time.

"You sure you want this?" His eyes were hooded as he

made quick work of the condom and eased the plump head of his cock where she needed him most. He had planned this.

"I've never been more sure." She lifted slightly before sinking down onto his impressive length. She hissed at the quick pinch of pain as he filled her.

"I guess so," he said, letting her run the show. "That's it, Melody, baby. You take what you want. What you need. I'm here to serve you."

She loved the sound of that.

She quickly found her rhythm, bouncing up and down so fast her breasts hurt from the violent thrusts. She couldn't stop. And when she started to slow, tightening around him, he took over, driving into her tight channel again and again. Her orgasm found her hard and fast, and she shuddered and called out as it ripped her open.

Aaron stilled, allowing her to ride out the glorious aftershocks.

"Christ, you're destroying me, baby," he said, feasting on her breast, waiting for her to float back down to earth. In that moment, there was no doubt in her mind. He owned her body and was quickly working his way into her soul.

It was dangerous, but she didn't care.

He pulled away, releasing her nipple in a loud pop before he flipped them over so she was now under him. Then he moved to her mouth. Devouring her inch-by-inch, he stirred something deep inside that brought her back to life. Soon, she began to roll her hips under him.

She loved the way his breathing grew ragged as he matched her movements. It wouldn't be long now. He pushed into her, slowly at first, then building, building. Finally, he couldn't move fast enough for her as he pushed her up and up until she was hanging over the edge. He was right there with her, and when she started to fall, she brought him, too.

This time he had to hold her as her climax vibrated through her, because she was a boneless puddle with no way of holding up her own body weight.

"It's okay, Mel," he soothed her. "I've got you."

She would've given anything for that to be true.

Chapter Twenty

Mel spent the evening combing through the schedule for Aaron's launch for the millionth time, not wanting to leave anything to chance. Turned out sex gave her laser focus and enormous energy. Who knew?

It'd been a week since the arrest, but they were so busy preparing for the launch it seemed like it had happened months ago. Mel kept working the plan with Tiffany, making great strides despite all the hiccups, and she stuck close to Genn, who was having her own issues at work. They'd become a real source of support for each other.

Poor Aaron was continuing to take questions about the arrest in the press interviews Mel had set up for him, but he took it like a champ and the questions became less and less frequent, especially once she started leaking information about a special love in his life. He didn't care for that part. At. All. But it was working. She'd have to ease him into the idea of the June Skye romance, but she still had a little time.

Mel and Aaron settled into an easy routine as they worked their way through the calendar, putting a big X through each day. It hurt each and every time she had to do it. Aaron made breakfast for them in the morning, and, when she was up for it, she'd take care of dinner. She'd just leave a note for him, listing all of the ingredients she needed, and he'd pick it up while she was at the office. Tonight, she was cooking.

They were now just five days away from the launch party…and seven from the Last Hurrah.

They both were getting jittery.

"I know, he does look a little like Jake Owen," Mel agreed, as she chatted up a blogger on the phone while she turned the shredded meat in the skillet. She was making pulled pork tacos this evening—her own take on a southern favorite.

"Tell me about your readership again," Mel said, gauging whether this particular press site was big enough to warrant the full multimedia kit. As Miranda kept reminding her, they were not cheap to produce.

"Whoa, really?" she said when the blogger rattled of the site's stats. This site was most definitely worthy. "Sure, I'll have my office FedEx a packet right away. And we'll see you at the launch? Excellent."

"Please tell me you're done for the day," Aaron said when he walked into the room. He was still a bit hesitant around her, always gauging her response, asking her permission for every little thing. Whether it stemmed from what'd happened with Jayden or he worried that the incident in Nashville had changed her opinion of him, she couldn't be sure. But he was so dang polite! No mistake, she liked this side of him, too. But Aaron when he wasn't holding back—that was her favorite.

"That was my last media call for the night." Mel did her happy dance booty shake. She was sick of walking on eggshells herself. It was time to get things back to normal.

"It smells so good in here, I don't want work-talk to ruin my appetite."

They'd both been working so hard that neither of them had the energy to do much in the evenings but talk, eat, and cuddle up on the couch with a movie. It was then that he'd reveal little bits and pieces to his past. Like last night when they watched a Nicolas Sparks' rodeo film.

"Reminds me of when Graham and I were kids," he'd said.

It was something so little, so seemingly insignificant, but it meant the world to her that he shared. That he felt safe with her.

She wondered if this was what married life would be like. Or was this just how it was with Aaron? It didn't matter because he had told her straight out that he didn't want a woman, a wife, or family. And she knew he had his hands full with his career and with his brother. She, on the other hand, was beginning to think she was ready for more.

"Did you see this?" She pointed to the calendar. "We only have a few of these dinners left."

"Don't remind me," he said as he raked his hands though his hair.

But Mel wasn't going to let it get her down. They only had a few days left and she wasn't going to waste them.

Even though there was still so much Mel didn't know about her roommate, she always paid attention to the things he did share—which gave her an idea of where she could take her cowboy before his world turned upside-down for the second time. They needed to get out and have some real fun.

She'd made the arrangements earlier that day, telling him only to dress casual and to be ready at seven.

"So where are you taking me tonight, ma'am?" he asked, hauling her onto his lap and nuzzling her neck. God, she loved when he did that that.

"It's a surprise." She quickly batted him away and stood up, her willpower waning. They needed to get out of there pronto, or there would be no going back. She knew how much he needed this, so she wouldn't succumb to his wicked ways, no matter how much she wanted to. That man and his magical hands.

"I thought you didn't like surprises," he said.

When did I tell him that?

"I don't like them," she agreed. "But that doesn't mean I don't like surprising others. Just give me a minute to change."

It was strange what they were able to pick up from each other in such a short amount of time. Like with Aaron—he didn't like violence on TV, not even the news, and he'd click that shit off without hesitation. He ate light in the morning and heavy at night—the opposite of what he should be doing, as she'd told him a dozen times already. He also didn't keep to a schedule, his wake and sleep patterns centered solely on his music, and, maybe most importantly, he needed white noise to sleep. She learned that when she took his fan into the living room and didn't return it before he went to bed.

"Don't change," he said, grabbing onto her legs before she could make her getaway. "I'm very fond of this look. What color do you call it?" He tugged on her skirt and snaked his hands underneath.

"Turquoise." Her eyes fluttered shut, the words scraping her throat on the way out.

"Pretty," he groaned, moving his hands inward. He played so dirty, but she could resist him if she wanted to. His fingers stretched closer. Must. Resist. Before he could get to her fine china, she jumped out of reach and took off running for her room.

"You're no fun," he called after her, but she didn't dare turn around. Couldn't risk it. She changed into a pair of jeans and a white button-down then tied her hair back in two loose pigtails.

Then she grabbed his cowboy hat from the closet and pushed him out the door.

"I feel like people are looking at me," Aaron said when they took their seats in the main grandstand, ready to watch the "most dangerous eight seconds in all of sports." Mel had to hand it to the rodeo marketers. That was a heckuva line.

"They're not looking at you," she said. Okay, she caught one or two glances their way, but she was hoping the Stetson and shades would help conceal him, at least a little bit. He needed to get used to the limelight again, but in small doses. Or at least learn how to have fun even if people were taking photos of his every move. "Don't worry about anyone else.

Let's just enjoy this."

"Do you know how long it's been since I've gone to the rodeo?" he asked with the sweetest smile she'd ever seen on his handsome face. He was even more striking without all those whiskers hiding his expressions.

"Tell me," she said. This was exactly what she was hoping for—a chance to connect and a way for him to let her in. She'd didn't have a lot of time left with him, and she at least wanted this before they went their separate ways.

She dismissed that thought, banishing it from their night. She wouldn't think about the future when they had the *now* together.

"It was the summer after I graduated high school," he said. "I was playing gigs all over our neighboring towns, saving up to get Graham and I out of our hometown. That godforsaken place. But after a particularly good week, I thought we deserved a treat. So I bought rodeo tickets and took Graham. I'm not ashamed to say it was about the coolest thing we'd ever seen. Growing up, we'd both had our share of farm work, caring for animals and such. But the rodeo was so much cooler."

"What was Graham's favorite part?" she asked, trying not to seem overeager as she took in every detail of his story.

"This," he said, looking over the stadium as the bull riders geared up for the show. "Adrenaline junkie, that one."

"What about you?"

He laughed, turning away from her. "I'm not going to say."

"Come on." She jabbed his ribs. "Don't be tease."

"I'm not," he said, meeting her gaze. "I just don't want to ruin my image as a rugged cowboy."

"Your secret's safe with me," she whispered. "Nobody here but you, me, and the ornery bull."

"Okay." He shook his head, taping his boot-clad feet on the aluminum riser "It was the babies."

"Babies? You mean the kids attending the rodeo?"

"No, though they were cute, too. I'm talking the animals. You know, the calves and horses and pigs. We watched a foal birthing and it was the most amazing thing I'd ever experienced. I know that probably sounds ridiculous."

Mel's heart squeezed, emotion bubbling up to the surface, but she didn't get the chance to say anything because the announcer's voice blared over the loudspeaker as he introduced the first rider.

It was probably for the best. So instead, she linked her hand in his.

Mel had been to the rodeo a ton of times as a kid. As part of her Miss Sweetwater duties she had to make appearances at all the local events, so for her it was more of a chore. She didn't have any heartwarming stories like Aaron did.

She imagined what it must've been like for the two brothers that summer. And she tried not to think about their life before they got out. She hoped to have him tell her that story some time, but tonight was about having fun and making memories.

They watched some of the best bull riders in the country fly out of the shoot on the most massive creatures she'd even seen. Mel was with Graham on this one — the bull riding was where it was at. But she also loved strolling through the different barns, walking hand-in-hand with Aaron. She knew his extra affection was probably because he was feeling melancholy, and she knew she shouldn't read more into it. That was easier said than done. So she let herself indulge…just for a while.

They ate pizza on a stick for dinner and a deep-fried candy bar for dessert. They even rode on the Ferris wheel in the midway.

Too soon, the sky turned dark and it was time to go back to reality.

Chapter Twenty-One

"Tell me," he demanded.

"No," she squealed as he threw her on the bed. They had quite the interesting conversation on the way home from the rodeo, and he simply had to have more information or he'd go nuts. They talked about what happened with Jayden and how it was for him on the road, and if he missed it, and all kinds of sexual questions that he wasn't prepared for but answered as best he could. And once she had the answers to all of her questions, he turned the tables to learn more about her.

"This is not something you can just blurt out, Aaron." She sat up but didn't leave the bed.

Good girl.

She had let him know earlier that one of the reasons she left Sweetwater was to gain experience in all things—work and play. What he hadn't known is that she hadn't really made much progress on the play side. It surprised him, considering how responsive and enthusiastic she'd been with him. It also was an enormous relief, which it shouldn't have been. She was not his, and he had no reason to feel one way or another about her sex life.

But when she mentioned that she had come up with a list of particulars that she wanted to check off before she headed home, he wanted to be the guy to help her.

"Let me at least hold on to some shred of my pride," she said. "This is embarrassing stuff."

How could he deny her request after what she did for him tonight? She said so much with that gesture. The memories and feelings and emotions had hit him hard. He couldn't believe she would plan that for him. He remembered mentioning his love for the rodeo one night in passing. He had no idea she'd been paying such close attention.

So yes, he should've given her a break regarding her little secret. But he wasn't going to. Not when the subject matter was this juicy. And there were other reasons, too. He wasn't a completely selfish bastard.

Mel wasn't going to be his roommate forever, and she'd already done so much for him. She definitely drew the short end of the stick in this arrangement, and he wanted to pay her back. In a big way.

"I will get it out of you, Melody Sharp." He joined her on the bed, tugging at her pigtails.

She cleared her throat and turned the most incredible shade of scarlet. Oh hell, this had to be good. He fixed his eyes on those plump lips, ready to hang on her every word.

"Okay," she said in a raspy voice that made him ache. Shit was getting serious. She looked at him from under her lashes. "So one of the things on my list is oral sex."

He interrupted her. "Hell, that shouldn't be anything new. It's the mainstay of every healthy relationship and even the unhealthy ones. Don't tell me you've been with guys who had an issue with it?

"You didn't let me finish," she said impatiently. "I mean doing it at the same time."

"You mean sixty-nine?" he asked.

"Yep, that's the one." She dropped back into bed, throwing a pillow over her head.

"You never did that with Teddy?" The name of her ex was rough on his throat.

She shook her head underneath the pillow, but he pulled it off. He needed to see her face as she said, "I always thought it sounded interesting, but well, it never worked out."

Never worked out? How was that even possible?

"Honey, it's not interesting, it's fucking fantastic. Filthy and erotic and hot. It can be pretty damn intimate, actually."

"What makes the difference, do you think?" He hated seeing the longing in her eyes, the shaken confidence in the way she held herself. This was a serious hang-up.

"Who you're with, I guess. And how much you're willing to give...and receive."

"Has it ever been intimate for you?"

"It's come close, I guess. But to be honest, most of my experience was on the road, as you know. Not exactly an intimate environment. These days, well, I really haven't gone to that point with anyone in a long time."

"Ah," she said, and he couldn't help the next words that fell out of his mouth.

"Not until you came along and squeezed your little ass into my life. With you, it'd be intimate. I think it'd be special.

Is that something you want to try with me?"

He wasn't sure who was more nervous about this proposition. She didn't say anything for several seconds, but he felt this was what she wanted and he wanted to be the man to give it to her. He had to be.

"It is," she said softly, in a very un-Mel-like manner. That was how important this was to her.

He thought it through. Damn, there were several ways they could go about it, and the most insanely erotic images flashed through his brain. *Calm the hell down.*

In the end he decided they'd take this slow—lying down with her on top. That way she could control the speed. The depth. The intensity.

"Come to me, Mel." He patted the bed between his legs. Just thinking about it had him quaking with need. He had to touch her.

"Hold on now," she told him, holding her place. "Let me get my bearings."

"I will help you set those bearings. Come."

She crawled over to him so that she was flanked by his thighs, her own legs draped over his. "So, how are we going to do this?" she asked, her voice trembling.

"I don't even want you to think about it, honey," he said as he unbuttoned her shirt. "I'll guide you. And you stop if anything is uncomfortable or you don't like it."

"Okay." Her voice steadied, bringing him great relief. He wanted her to enjoy every second of them pleasuring each other.

He slowly undressed her despite their awkward positions—but this was nothing compared to what they'd be doing next. It was best to prepare her ahead of time.

Her shirt came off first, rather easily, as did his. He flicked the front clasp of her bra. It fell open, giving him an eyeful. He couldn't get enough of her breasts. The gentle slope of them, sitting high on her chest. The weight of them in his hands. Her pert, rosy nipples. He pulled one into his mouth until she shuddered. Her reactions gave him the biggest rush.

"Lift your butt, sweetheart," he told her, continuing his quest to have her naked and on top of him as soon as possible. He pulled her jeans down to her knees, taking her panties along for the ride, and then freed each leg. She giggled as he maneuvered her.

Just wait, little Mel.

She helped him do the same with his boxers, but it wasn't nearly as pretty.

"Okay, now scoot down there on the bed and kneel," he told her gently, trying to keep his enthusiasm in check. He had to hold it together, or he wasn't going to last more than two minutes. And he wasn't going to ruin this for her. But damn, she was so beautiful waiting for him. He joined her, on his knees at first so he could feast on her mouth. He wanted her drenched by the time they began.

Skimming his thumb over her bottom lip, he made her open for him so she could wet his finger. She complied without question and was rewarded in kind when that finger reached her center.

He swept his tongue into her mouth as he worked his finger at her core, circling. She moaned into this kiss as he claimed her with each stroke, each touch, pushing his way further inside. She became almost pliant as he thoroughly worked her over.

It was time.

Breaking the kiss, his tongue drew a path down her body, savoring her sweet taste as she bowed into him. When he reached her center, he parted her with his tongue, consumed by the addictive scent of her arousal. She was just as he wanted her—all warm, wet heat.

He flipped onto his back, and she tensed as he worked his way between her legs so she was straddling his head.

"I'm going to start now, Melody." He gripped her thighs, bringing the part he craved closer to his mouth. "You can join me when you're ready."

Chapter Twenty-Two

Mel was convinced she looked like a porn star. This was, by far, the most precariously filthy position she'd ever put herself in. And she rather liked it.

She took a breath to acclimate to the intense stimulation going on down below, and then summoned the courage to take a look. She almost passed out—it was that hot. If she lifted just slightly, she could catch a glimpse of Aaron's pink tongue. Her head was swimming in lust, and she wanted more.

It was her turn.

She lowered her torso, bracing her weight on her hands as she brought herself level with Aaron's beautiful cock. It was true that most women she knew would never put those two words together, but they had never been up close and personal with Aaron Major's most prized possession.

"Ahh," she cried out, as something unexpected happened. When she shifted position, her angle changed, which meant so did Aaron's mouth. He went deeper, reaching the most pleasurable of spots. He chuckled and she felt the vibrations deep in her bones. Oh my God, she needed to hurry.

She didn't waste any time with foreplay, but rather took him fast and hard in one swift thrust until his length hit the back of her throat. His hips almost bucked them off the bed. She did it again, but slower this time, bringing him in inch by inch, savoring his taste, his smell, and his response as she changed the speed and pressure. She studied him, recording each reaction, each move that made him crazy with desire.

And as she focused on pleasing Aaron, he was rocking her freaking world. She leaned into him as he drove his tongue deeper with each thrust.

She felt the pull low in her belly and tried to shut it down as she stroked her cowboy with her mouth and hand. She'd never felt closer to another soul, and understood what he meant about intimacy. She'd also never felt more desired, and she didn't want this to end until they drained every ounce of pleasure from each other.

The feeling was indescribable, pure ecstasy building and building with the promise of more. The room filled with the fragrance of cedar and soap, spice and sex—a delicious combination that made her head fuzzy.

Aaron slid his hands to the inside of her legs, spreading her wider. Then he gripped her bottom and slammed her onto his mouth. He rocked her on his tongue, and there was no warning for what came next. She shattered, tensing and tightening, as he helped her ride it out in slow, rough strokes. In the very next breath, he followed her with three vicious pumps, before his release.

They stayed that way, wrapped in each other until the

pleasure faded.

Aaron, tenderly, gingerly, flipped them onto their sides.

He kissed her shins, her knees, paying special attention to her thighs, hips, belly, and breasts along the way. She climbed on top of him then, and buried her face in the crook of his neck, breathing in that woodsy scent she adored. She knew what he meant about the intensity of this particular act. She felt it in her bones.

She got up to get them both some water, walking past her makeshift office in the kitchen, where the bold print on the planner made her heart drop.

They had less than a week left together.

The two of them slept like the dead that night, so the knock on the door the next morning was unwelcome. And Mel wouldn't deny that after what they shared, she wanted time with Aaron to decompress. She'd grown to depend on him.

The man was addicting. It wasn't only that he jumpstarted her libido. He also had this way about him that made her feel like anything was possible. She craved to see the world through his eyes, how he processed the things going on around him, and then turned them into his art. He was soothing and deep and insanely interesting. And he seemed to be enamored of her.

"I'll get it," she said, getting up to answer the door.

"Get rid of them," Aaron growled. "Whoever it is."

Jayden's visit had left a dark cloud in his wake, and she cursed him for the wedge he drove between them. Aaron was still pissed as hell about the whole thing. And forget about the Nashville scandal. Yeah, Jayden had made it abundantly clear to the media that Aaron was in no way connected to Toby's bad behaviors, but that didn't mean either of them had completely forgiven their old friend. She wasn't sure if it was what Jayden did or what it reminded him of that upset Aaron so much. But it was obvious he was in no hurry to have another guest.

Mel opened the door to a very tall and incredibly handsome younger guy. Too young for her, but something about him made her stand up and take notice.

He crinkled up his nose, and looked her over slowly. He had dark eyes…deep and penetrating just like someone else she knew. Recognition dawned. He had a thinner, lankier build, but the same unruly hair. It was Aaron's brother. It had to be. He was at least a few years younger than she was, which made perfect sense.

"Hi, I'm Mel," she told him. "Are you here for Aaron?" He didn't say a word or meet her eyes again. He focused on her lips instead, then he nodded in response.

"Aaron," Mel called behind her. "There's someone here to see you." She kept her hand on the door, just in case the kid wasn't welcome. Of course, Aaron could light up a Christmas tree whenever Graham's name came up, but he'd also been so closed-lipped about him, so she'd stopped prying.

"Well, are you going to stand there all day checking out my brother or are you going to let him in?" Aaron asked in that playful way of his.

"I wasn't checking him out," Mel argued.

"I'm kidding, Mel," he teased.

She pushed at his arms, hoping to throw him off balance.

He didn't budge.

"Hey, bro." Aaron surprised her by using sign language as he spoke. "This is Melody, my publicist…and my roommate. Mel, this is my brother Graham."

The signing caught her completely off guard. Why wouldn't it? Aaron never mentioned his brother was hearing impaired. Not that he should have or anything, but she hated surprises.

"I see the resemblance," she said, searching the files in her brain for American Sign Language she learned in high school. Damn him, if he'd shared this information, she could've been prepared.

Graham signed something after her comment, but his hands moved too fast for her to follow.

Aaron spoke for him. "He's says he's much better looking."

"Nice to meet you," Mel signed, at an embarrassingly slow pace. At least she hoped that was what she said. That brain file of hers was covered in dust.

Graham's face pulled into a huge grin, but it was Aaron who lit up the place.

"You sign?" he asked with wide eyes.

"I took ASL in high school," she said. "I'm very rusty."

As it turned out, Graham got permission from his teachers to take a few extra days for his brother's launch party. He'd come in on the Greyhound from his boarding school in Boston.

"Why didn't you tell me?" Aaron said. "I could've flown you here or at least picked you up from the bus station."

"I wanted to surprise you," Graham signed and said with a soft, clipped voice, laced with the tiniest of impediment. It was probably for her benefit, so she'd know what was going on, but he didn't seem comfortable speaking.

"Mission accomplished." Aaron moved to grab one of his bags from the hall. "Now get in here so you can tell me all about that fancy school of yours."

Mel's heart squeezed as she watched them together, and soon everything started to make sense—Aaron's protective nature, his temporary cash flow issue... One look at him now, the way he was with his brother, and she knew he'd do anything for him. And most likely already was.

"**D**ude, I didn't know," Graham said to his brother, using the clearest speech Aaron ever heard, and he almost fell out of his chair. His voice was deeper though, even more than it had been a few months ago, and it was pure music to Aaron's ears.

Mel had left to pick up some bagels for breakfast, so the two of them could have the chance to catch up, and he was thankful.

"I don't want to put you out with your woman here," he said, and Aaron laughed. Okay, that was a little weird having his little brother comment on his woman. For all he knew, the kid had a girlfriend of his own. Really, he didn't care what he talked about, as long as he talked. Graham's special schooling had be the best money Aaron ever spent.

"Don't be stupid," he said. "She'll stay in my bed. That spare room is yours, you know that."

Aaron had always made a home for his brother no matter where he was. Graham had even spent some time on tour with him one summer, before things got out of control.

He hated to think where he'd be without him.

"So there is something going on with the two of you?" Graham quirked a brow.

"Something." Aaron nodded.

Graham smiled, clearly happy to with that news. "She seems…good."

Goodness was about the highest compliment you could get from the Major boys, because they hadn't seen much of it after their daddy died. "Don't get all sappy on me," Aaron joked. "I have no idea *where* it's going or even *if* it's going."

Graham looked great. Healthy, muscular, like he was ready for college. He was. He'd already been accepted to a private university in Florida. Aaron couldn't help but beam with pride over that. Graham would be the first in the family with a degree, not that there was anyone around other than Aaron to take note.

"What about you?" Aaron asked. "Anyone interest you at school?"

"There was someone," he said. Aaron couldn't get over how fucking amazing he sounded, but he didn't want to make a big deal of it. He worked to keep him talking instead.

Graham rarely used his voice. Around Aaron, sure. But not many other people. Public school had been hard enough for Graham, and his speech was one more thing that made him different, one more thing for the kids to tease him about. They took his voice, and Aaron wanted to beat their little asses. He had, in fact, gotten into a few scuffles with parents on his brother's behalf. After that, even Aaron didn't hear from Graham much.

And there wasn't a lot they could do about it back then. Their financial situation was always dire and unstable once his mama stopped singing. The state made sure Graham had access to education, hearing tests, and adequate hearing aids, but between his mom not really giving a shit, and their rural location, Graham missed out on the consistent therapy that would have made his life a lot easier. But since he'd been away at his new school, he'd had the best speech therapy every day, and Aaron got him the most advanced hearing aids money could buy. The change in his brother over the last year was incredible, but it'd taken a toll on Aaron's bank account, and now there was college to consider. That was why Aaron was determined to make his music career work on a commercial level, because he needed that paycheck.

At one time, he had all the money he needed for Graham, but that fund had run dry, thanks to his mama. She had spent hundreds of thousands of dollars—of Aaron's money—those first few years after he was signed. Lavish trips, cars, jewelry, you name it. He was partly to blame. When the money started to trickle in, he'd use it to buy his mama's attention and affection. At least until Graham's needs became more apparent. That's when his brother took precedent over everything and everyone. He had no guilt over that decision.

Chapter Twenty-Three

When Mel came back to the apartment with the bagels, Aaron was on the couch playing his guitar, while
Graham sat on the floor with his hand resting on the back
of the instrument. She assumed it was his way of listening to
the music. It was beautiful.

"That's my favorite," Graham signed and spoke in that
quiet voice of his, and Mel told him she agreed. It was easily
the best song on the album. She was impressed how well he
knew his brother's music.

"Come on now." Mel stood where Graham could see
her lips. "Time to eat."

The three of them sat in the living room that morning,
drinking coffee, eating bagels, and listening to Aaron play.
She couldn't think of a better way to spend the day.

But when her phone went off, and she caught the caller
ID, her stomach dropped, shooting her mood all to hell.

"Everything okay?" Aaron asked.

"Fine," she lied. "Just something I have to take care of right quick."

It was a text message from Teddy. Since she never responded to his email, he decided to take a new approach. Surprisingly, she was ready to answer.

Okay, she replied.

She went back into the room to rejoin Aaron and Graham, but couldn't fully be in the moment, not with her meeting with Teddy at the forefront of her mind. And that really pissed her off.

M el had been burning the midnight oil in the final days leading up to the launch, and it had Aaron worried. He hated to see her working so hard on his behalf, but he knew she was under the gun, too.

She needed her former title reinstated before she went home. Not that anyone would necessarily find out about the demotion. Though who knew—he'd lived in many small towns and there were always a few people stirring the pot and bringing up business that wasn't their own.

Aaron had a mind to call Miranda himself, but Mel would be mortified, and he couldn't do that to his girl.

His girl.

Shoot, he wasn't looking forward to her leaving. It killed him just thinking about it. That's why he was hoping she'd take the evening and come out with him and Graham.

He bought three tickets to the Brave's game, just in case.

While they waited for her to come home, Graham took residence in the best spot in the living room, as he always did. Man, it felt good to have him there. He was watching some celebrity game show with the closed captioning turned on, laughing along with the obnoxious host and yelling out the answers, beating the buzzer each time.

"Dude, once your album hits, you totally have to do this show," he said.

Aaron did a jerk-off motion with his hand. Being around his brother always brought back the idiocies of adolescence.

But when Mel walked in, he stopped immediately. Everything about her made him want to be a better man.

"How are the Major boys this fine evening?"

"We're getting ready for the Braves game," Graham said. "You in?"

"Oh, that sounds perfect," she said, depositing her computer bag at the campaign headquarters. Now that was something Aaron wasn't going to miss, he couldn't wait to get that shit off his table. "We could order some fried chicken from Kenny's. It'd be heaven."

"No, darlin'," Aaron interrupted her. "I've got tickets for all of us. So go get changed—it's a seven ten game time, and we can eat at the stadium."

"I can't." She hung her head. "I was going to wait to tell you, but I have a few things to add to the campaign."

"No. No more." He was adamant. "We can't handle any more. Just look at this calendar for fucks' sake."

"Don't worry," she said, scribbling some new items down. "This is all me. Miranda left me a message today, the warm soul that she is, and baring any disasters at the launch, I will have my old job reinstated."

"Oh, honey, that's great news." He picked her up and squeezed, unable to contain himself, and they both seemed to melt into each other. Graham cleared his throat from the other room—little prick.

Still, he was thrilled she was going to see the fruit of her labor. And this way, she had choices. She could even stay in Atlanta if she wanted to. It was something he tried not to think about, but now it was a real possibility.

"There's just one other thing I need to do," Mel added.

Of course there was. It seemed to be Miranda's way. "What is it?"

"Warm up your label. We'd like a testimonial from them, and Rita's been keeping me at a bus-length distance."

"What? Why didn't you tell me?"

"Because that's not your job to handle it. It's mine. Miranda knows that, and knowing her, it's some kind of test. I have to learn to play in the sandbox with the big boys and girls."

"Is that another Frankieism?" He hadn't forgotten her drunken diatribe the night of her eviction, after she'd attended the Frankie Finch seminar.

She smiled. "You bet your ass it is. You guys go have fun. And I'll just work on the label stuff while you're out."

Graham laughed at the stupid game show and it was such an amazing sound. He and Mel looked over at him at the same time, just as the show's host asked, "Next question for the win: what's something that looks better on a woman than a man?"

And before he could beg Mel one more time to come with them, she ran out to the living room and signed "boobs" before the game show buzzer went off. Graham laughed again, so hard Aaron thought he might have peed himself.

Leave it to Mel—it was the number one answer.

Chapter Twenty-Four

"Mel," Aaron called out. "It's time to get moving."

"Hold your horses, I'm coming," she called back. As if she'd she didn't plan this event down to the second. She was heading out first and then had a car ready to pick up Aaron and the band shortly after. He was nervous, and she was happy about that. A little adrenaline always did the body good. As for her? She was ready and steady. Especially once she learned Miranda was called away for other business. She'd be so much better without the Ice Queen monitoring her every move.

Tonight, for once, Mel wasn't wearing a lick of color. She wanted to blend into the background ensuring everything was perfect. Her charcoal-colored dress was understated; her hair pulled back; her makeup light with the exception of smoky eyes. She looked like her boss might at an event.

"Wow," Graham said in his voice when she walked into the room, and a lump the size of Texas lodged in her throat.

The past few days with Aaron and Graham had been the most fun she'd had…ever. Growing up with girls, she didn't get a chance to see the way brothers interacted with one another. The bravado, their lazy style, the way they could insult each other one minute and be laughing their asses off the next. She found them fascinating.

Aaron cleared his own throat. "Yeah, wow," he said, his eyes raking over her body. It made her shiver. "You look finer than frog hair."

"Be still my heart." She laughed. "Stop with your sweet talk."

"Just calling 'em like I see 'em."

He pulled her in for a long, consuming kiss that made her vision blur and the apex of her thighs ache. Damn him. Graham made himself scarce.

"You go out there tonight and kill it," she said. "You deserve this moment so much."

"So do you, Mel." He stroked her arms. "You've worked so hard and I could've never done this without you."

"Save your compliments, because it's not over yet."

Pray was perfect. Dim light. Candles flickering on the tables. The Man in Black playing his subdued tracks in the background—a little homage to Aaron's idol. At the head of the room—the altar—a stage was set up for the band: a drum set, an upright base, mic stands, stools. It was a sparse set for Aaron's minimalist sound.

Mel had seen to every last detail. Energy hummed under her skin, and it wasn't just because it was *him*. Sure, that was part of it. But this launch, for this artist? She would've done anything to ensure it was a success.

She ran into Rita on her way to check-in with the caterers. She'd never met her in person, but her research told her exactly who she needed to look for.

"Rita." She held out a hand. "So nice to meet you in person. I'm Melody Sharp."

"Ah yes," she said. "You should know, the red wine is terrible. Really subpar."

"Strange," she said, nodding to the caterers to start circulating the hors d'oeuvres. "I had Miranda's personal friend, who happens to be a sommelier, approve the list. I'll be sure to tell her what you said."

"Don't bother," Rita brushed her off, looking for someone, anyone, in the room to save her.

"We're here to support Aaron, not critique wine, right?" Mel didn't wait for an answer.

People were beginning to filter in now. Middle-aged men in hats and boots, younger ones covered in facial hair and ink, ladies in simple dresses and slacks. It was a modest crowd, but there was a crackle in the air. There always was with so many creative people in one space.

"What do you need, babe?" Genn came up behind her and wrapped an arm around Mel's shoulder.

Mel beamed when she turned around to see Genn and Tiffany in their best-dressed glory. Genn opted for casual elegance in her black wrap dress and boots, and Tiffany was a little more young and funky with her leather pants. The best part? They came bearing good news.

Things were on track with June Skye, and Aaron Major was trending on social media.

"I can't believe I'm going to say this, but I think we're good," Mel said. "So you two just go and have a great time and an extra dozen drinks for me. Oh, wait, not that many. I have a surprise for both of you later, and you'll want to remember it."

Mel hugged them and went to the front podium where two enormous bodyguards had been posted, and looked over the guest list one more time. It was impressive. Then again, she'd sent Aaron's single along with the invite. Who could *not* show after they heard that brilliance? All invites were personally delivered to anyone who was anyone in the music industry, not to mention the underground scene, which could spread the word faster than any radio station. They hit every avenue of outreach, because Aaron's music was ageless, timeless. He was the real deal.

She counted thirty members of the media on the list, dozens of producers and songwriters, a handful of major recording artists and tons of up-and-comers. And one name in particular that jumped from the page.

Aaron would be thrilled with the last part of her plan: the surprise guest. Until he knew the real reason why she was coming. But it was necessary. He needed some June Skye magic to reinstate his Country Card. No matter how much it pained her to throw him into the arms of another woman—even if it was just for show.

She'd contemplated telling him about the "guest" sooner, and she'd even hemmed and hawed over revealing the motivation behind her presence, but what if she didn't show? That scandal in Nashville had been a hard blow to Aaron, and if some of the greats of country music—his old peers—started turning their backs on him, she didn't think it would help his confidence.

She continued going through her last minute checklist. She'd been on the phone and working the crowd, so by the time she checked the clock, they were only minutes away from Aaron's appearance. The room was close to capacity when Miranda arrived.

Mel beelined to the Ice Queen. So much for her being unavailable this evening. Come to think of it, she should've known that Miranda never would've missed this event. Not for the publicity it garnered for Elite, and not for the chance to land more clients.

"So, how do you think I did?" she whispered to her boss as she shuttled her around the VIPs, making introductions to the few people Miranda didn't know.

"We'll see, Melody," she said. "We'll see."

Not the ringing endorsement she was hoping for. So on that cautious note, Mel squared her shoulders and decided, come hell or high water, she'd make this night a success.

Miranda mingled and Mel snuck off to the dressing room. Aaron and the guys had to be here by now. The car she ordered should've deposited them at the back entrance fifteen minutes ago.

Without wasting another second, she went to check on her man of the hour—correction, *the* man of the hour. *The* man.

The space behind the former pulpit had been converted into a dressing room. Aaron had enough jokes about that to fill a book.

When she walked in, the sight made her heart dance in her chest.

You'd think she'd be immune to the man by now. She'd

seen him naked for the love of Pete. Didn't matter. She'd thought Teddy was something back in the day, but he had nothing on the cowboy. Her stomach turned at the mention of her ex, who she'd been thinking more and more about since his email.

She shook away the unpleasant thought and drank in the sight in front of her, starting at the bottom and working her way up. Black boots that were more biker than cowboy—he made that decision on his own, and she liked that. She liked it very much. Dark jeans that covered what she knew were insanely muscular legs. Legs that could hold them both up… if the opportunity presented itself. Her eyes continued their perusal, and she noticed that he was warming up to the idea of more flash in the pan—yep, that denim was decidedly more snug than anything else in his closet and it held him perfectly. She expelled a long breath and shuddered.

"Are you quite finished?" he said, with a rasp to his tone that she didn't recognize.

"No," she whined. "I only reached your waist. Nice belt by the way."

"Thanks," he said, the smile back in his voice.

"Now I have to go back and start from the beginning," she quipped.

"Come here." He reached for as she quickly surveyed the rest of him. Gray V-neck T-shirt that had the perfect amount of give. A cool silver pendant on a leather rope, which filled in the space in the V and made Mel growl. She wanted a better look at that golden skin.

The guys dispersed and settled into the adjoining room, giving them space. She said hello and even acknowledged Jayden with an appreciative nod, before she caught Aaron coming in for a kiss.

"How's it looking out there?" he asked before finding her lips. She gave her mouth to him, but he didn't consume it like he usually did. His kisses were soft and searching. He was looking for comfort, not heat, so that was what she gave him as she entwined her hands with his.

"It's perfect out there, darlin'," she told him. "The only thing missing is you. More importantly, how are you feeling?"

"Okay, I think."

"Well, in case you didn't realize it when I assaulted you with my eyes, you look like a fucking country god, so no worries there. And your voice completely wrecks me."

He frowned.

"Seriously, are you okay?"

"Yeah, I am." He took a seat in one of the overstuffed chairs and Mel sat on the arm. She needed to be close. "This just brings back a lot of memories."

"That's okay," she assured him, messing with his hair. Lord, she loved his hair. "This is a full-circle moment. You weren't ready before, did it for the wrong reasons, but you've grown and you have even more to say now with your music. They're going to love you."

"I don't care about their love," he said. "Yes, I appreciate anyone who cares about my music or wants to hear me sing, but I don't need that adoration like I did before. My circle is a small one and I only need love from a very few."

He stroked her cheek, and no matter how she tried to stop it, hope leaked in that maybe they could have more together. Maybe she could join that tiny circle.

"All right, boys," Rita came barreling in. Oh, she was exhausting. "It's time to get his show on the road."

"It's okay, Rita," Aaron said. "I think Mel's got this."

"No," Mel said. "She right. It's time."

O nce the women left, it was just the guys again. They had so many people coming in and out of the dressing room the entire time, that they really hadn't had much time to themselves. And he and Jayden had been trying to stay out of each other's way.

It had been the same way at the rehearsals. Plus, because of his stupid rules at the onset of his comeback, Aaron hadn't wanted to connect with the band. Maybe because he was afraid of how much he missed it, playing and collaborating with other people. It was a vulnerable thing to depend on someone else, to get up on stage and trust that the person next to you had your back. And what if they didn't?

But those were really his issues stemming from old wounds, and he was realizing that the band wasn't always the problem...then or now.

He was.

And maybe it was time to put all that shit behind him and trust someone for a change. The five of them talked through the set, tuning the instruments and marking some pieces of the show, and hell, it was fun.

"Aaron." Jay must've felt his wall come down, because he finally addressed the elephant in the room. "Dude, I'm so sorry for what went down with Toby. I've been wanting to talk to you about it, but didn't know what to say. But honestly, I had no idea, man. I would never risk you like that."

"What do you mean you had no idea?" Aaron asked.

The fool went on television and took full responsibility.

"What I said on TV was a lie," Jayden admitted. "But people would not have believed you weren't involved unless someone came forward to take the blame. It was the only way to get the shit off you. And it was about time I try to do that."

"Hang on," Aaron said, as he heard Casey Black's voice from out on the stage.

"Forget it man," Jay waved him off. "I don't want to talk about any more shit from the past. I'm so tired of it, aren't you?"

"Hell yes," he said, and with those two words he swore he could breathe a little easier.

"Okay." Jayden patted him on the back. "Then let's just go out and kill this thing and start our future."

And that's exactly what they did. They listened as a legend introduced them, and then went on stage and played their hearts out.

It wasn't such a bad way to live.

Chapter Twenty-Five

"Ladies and Gents, it's great to see y'all outside of Nashville for a change, to celebrate with one of Georgia's newest residents." Casey Black made the introductions, and Mel could only imagine what Aaron was thinking when he heard his voice. Casey Black was in the same league as Johnny Cash as far as Aaron was concerned.

Once Mel secured Mr. Black to do the opening remarks, she kept it a secret. It had been hell. But the way these guys changed their calendars, she couldn't risk any disappointment if he couldn't make it. Still, she wished she were backstage right now to see Aaron's face.

Graham's expression was almost as good. He was right up front so he could read the legend's lips, and feel the stage once the music started. He shook his head and patted his heart. "You are awesome," he mouthed. His smile was so bright it made Mel weepy.

Boy, she was in so much trouble.

"I've already had the chance to listen to the songs he's going to play for you tonight, and let me tell ya something—they are going to blow you away. *He's* going to blow you away. Now, I met him when he was part of The Major Band, but now that he's out on his own—with the help of his partner in crime, Jayden Brink—he has a whole new feel. A new look. A new sound. And one helluva new story. Let's bring him to the stage…Aaron Major."

He took to the stage and Mel heard the ladies in the audience release a breathy sigh in unison. She knew it was going to happen, but still wasn't ready for it.

For the past few weeks, Mel had had him all to herself. But the time had come to release him into the world and let him fly. Why did it have to happen so fast?

Aaron stood at the mic and began belting out the lyrics of a dark, almost haunting song. Graham stood next to the amp that the guys pushed to the edge of the stage, and he felt the music. She wondered if he could feel the hurt that Aaron pushed from his lungs, because Mel sure could. And by the look of the crowd, who seemed completely mesmerized in the moment, they did too.

As the band continued to play, the mood of the songs lightened and the crowd responded accordingly. Couples danced, people talked, and everyone raved about Aaron.

Mel chatted up the journalists and bloggers and made sure they had everything they needed. Some wanted to schedule follow-up interviews, others needed his headshots, and she took care of it. But she had one more thing to do.

"Hey there, Ceecee." She greeted her favorite vlogger. "How'd you like the show?"

"Shit." Ceecee rubbed her tatted arms. "I've had goose

bumps all night. It was amazing. And I've been meaning to tell you, damn fine work on the promo vids."

Mel caught Tiffany's eye and waved. "About that," she said. "I want to introduce you to the woman responsible for those. Tiffany—" Mel pulled her over to join them. "This is Ceecee, vlogger extraordinaire."

"Oh, I know who she is," Tiffany said.

"Ceecee, this is the woman in charge of our promo vids. She just graduated from GSU."

"Really?" Ceecee said, quickly sweeping Tiff away. Mel knew Ceecee had an open spot on her team that would be perfect for her favorite intern.

Tiffany mouthed, *I love you*, to Mel as she pulled her away.

Mel moved over to Rita, who was chatting up the mayor of Atlanta. Mel had to pat herself on the back for that one, though she never thought he'd show. She wanted Aaron involved in the community, and she wanted to build some good will. So she stopped by to say hello.

"Mr. Mayor, we're so happy you could make it," Mel said.

"I was happy to receive the invitation," he said. "Great show."

"Aaron's amazing, right?"

"A big talent there," he said.

"You know," Mel interjected, and she swore she saw Rita roll her eyes. "I've heard about your new pre-K music program for the underprivileged kids in the city and wanted to let you know that Aaron is a big supporter. So if you ever need a face for the cause, or another spokesperson, I'm sure he'd be happy to help."

"That would be fantastic," he said. "And you are?"

"Melody Sharp, Aaron's PR manager." She handed him her card. "Please, let me know if there's anything you need."

Almost done.

Though she was exhausted with all the schmoozing and talking, she was actually having an incredible time. She laughed, thinking about how much Aaron would hate it. The band started a new song, and she had to stop for a minute and take him in. She was so proud of him tonight. Watching him on stage made everything else fade into the background. Once she did pull her eyes away from Aaron's jeans, she noticed Graham was missing from his spot by the amp.

It didn't take long to locate him. As she scanned the room, she saw that he had made his way over to an up-and-coming young singer named Avery Jay, who also lived in Atlanta. She'd been posting on social media all night, shaking her little butt off. Apparently, Mel wasn't the only one who noticed.

She looked on as he asked Avery to dance. She wondered if he used his voice or mouthed the words, it didn't matter. Point was, he was going for what he wanted. Avery laughed and did a little hair flip that meant she was definitely interested. Mel looked to the stage and caught Aaron's face, silently asking, *Are you seeing this?* He followed and his eyes went wide once he zeroed in on his brother.

Graham pulled Avery onto the dance floor with the confidence that his brother possessed, and he handled the girl in much the same way that Aaron did her. Gentle, but firm, with a coolness that only these two guys could pull off. Graham held Avery in that same possessive way, wrapping her tight but holding her hand against his chest, tapping on it to create his own beat. Mel went a little melty.

From the stage, Aaron shook his head with a grin that would be forever locked in Mel's brain. Because in that moment she knew, without out a doubt, that'd she'd fallen utterly, painfully in love with him.

And that made what came next even more difficult.

June Skye was class and stardom and power all rolled into one. She was closer to Aaron's age than Mel was, with long dark hair that was perfectly mussed in a sexy, effortless fashion. She was trendy and had style that Mel could never pull off—clashing patterns, tall boots, and a funky sapphire coat with a cream-colored long leather vest. And she was a country music darlin'.

She fit in this world, where Mel clearly did not. And her name was June for fuck's sake. It was kismet.

As Aaron wrapped up his set, she knew it was time to make her move. June was the hottest thing on the scene right now, and she liked to be out and loved to be photographed. From the way her eyes were eating up Aaron on stage, Mel's little scheme would be a cinch to pull off.

Mel had already talked to Rita about it, even after she made her threats, who of course loved the idea. She had the feeling Rita's bark was worse than her bite. And June's manager was on board as well. A few days, a few tweets, some leaked photos of them together. It was the perfect timing for him to work the romance angle. After tonight, the doors to his future would be wide open.

"June," Mel finally made her way to make the introductions. "I'm Melody Sharp, Aaron's publicist."

"Right," she extended a hand. "You are the brain behind the Skye/Major connection. Damn, I tried pulling together one of those celebrity names for us, but I can't seem to find a combination that works. Oh well, nobody will care when they get a look at Aaron Major all grown up and filled out. He's a real star, that one."

"He is," Mel agreed, trying to ignore the knot in her stomach.

"So, how far is he into his set?" she asked, surveying the room and posturing like someone might take a photo at any moment—which, Mel immediately noticed, some of the bloggers were.

"Almost finished," she said.

"Great, I'll have my assistant start tweeting." She waved to a mousy girl, who stood a few paces behind, her thumbs flying over the keys on her phone. "He's really amazing," June added.

"Right?" Melody hated this will every fiber of her being. But she couldn't dwell on it. She had one last thing to do, before she went out and broke her own dang heart.

How she detesting adulting.

She found Genn, took her by the hand and said, "Get ready."

Then the two of them stopped right in front of the Ice Queen. Mel made her introductions and sang Genn's praises. Now it was up to her new friend to take it to the next level. Was she serious about leaving the office of Neanderthals for something better?

They'd find out soon enough.

But before she could slip away, Miranda led her away for a moment.

"Superb," she said out of the blue.

"I'm sorry, ma'am, what do you mean?" Mel asked.

"Oh, Melody." She sighed. "You really need to keep up. I'm answering your earlier question regarding my assessment of this event. My answer is: superb."

Mel couldn't move, couldn't talk, for what felt like minutes. She had no idea that word was even in her boss's vocabulary. And to use it about something Mel did? She didn't know what to say.

"Thank you, Miranda," she said, when she could finally talk. And once the blood came back to her legs, she almost ran away.

Because the Ice Queen would have a fit if she saw Mel cry.

"Aaron." Mel pulled him offstage as soon as they finished. "This is June Skye."

"I know who she is," he said, giving Mel the evil eye. What was she up to now? He wasn't sure, but he'd play along. "Nice to meet you, June. I loved *Get the Girl*."

Aaron wasn't usually so accommodating, but he had to give Mel what she wanted tonight, especially after she worked so hard. The evening was epic, and how she got all these people to come out and see him, he'd never know.

"Thanks." June beamed. "I've been a fan of yours forever."

"You look too young to be any fan of mine," he said, and she really did. Though sometimes he had to remember he was just a kid when he went on the road the first time.

"Well, aren't you the sweetest," June cooed, grabbing his arm as a few warning bells went off in is head.

Mel shifted her stance, pushing him closer to the country pop icon—which of course, he hated. He didn't lie when he said he liked her song. He did, but that was the only one. He wasn't what'd you'd call a fan of the rest of her work. His tastes generally required more substance.

Mel took out that damn phone again and started clicking. "Twitter," she said by way of explanation. She then backed away to give them some space. He didn't like her in the shadows, blending into the background. She should be out there with him, at his side.

"Guess they want us to been seen together," June said. Okay, she now had his full attention.

"Oh really?" This was news.

"Yeah, my manager is all about cross-promo with other artists. She has me party-jumping almost every night."

"Interesting," he bristled. "Apparently mine is all about secrecy." And his publicist, too. Once he caught Mel's attention, all it took was one look to tell her he wasn't pleased.

She became suddenly very interested in something in the other direction.

Little snake.

"I'm sorry," June said, also catching onto his irritation. "This is really embarrassing. But I want you to know the promo thing isn't why I came."

Right.

"I would've been here either way, because I do love your music."

"It's okay, June. I'm not upset with you. Not at all. And okay, if this is what they want, we can do that. Help each other out." He had a few ideas of his own from time to time.

"Exactly my thoughts." She ran a boney hand down his chest.

He cringed, but was almost happy when he saw Mel's eye go wide from the other side of the room.

Hey, you asked for it, sweetheart.

"June, what do you say you join me for one on the next set?" he asked.

"Don't you tease me now, Mr. Major."

"I wouldn't dream of it."

Chapter Twenty-Six

He had to admit it was a little fun messing with Mel. He brought June up on stage and pretended they'd known each other for years. They sang a few tracks off his album and one hideous song off of hers, then mugged for the cameras and even toasted champagne together.

Mel looked about as worried as a virgin on prom night—the same way he'd been feeling lately. Their arrangement was about to end and he had no idea where they'd go from here. All he knew was that he didn't want her to leave. And not only just for his sake.

She was great at her job, great in this city, and he didn't want her to sell out, or to make a decision based on what other people thought about her. He also didn't want her to make a decision based on him, which is why he held back, not saying a word to anyone about the way he'd fallen for her—goddamn ass over teakettle.

They ended on one hell of a high note, getting the entire

crowd pumped up before sending them on their way. At the end of it all, he was exhausted and just wanted to go home, hang with his brother, catch SportsCenter, and then go to bed with his woman. It was his idea of heaven.

"Did you get everything you needed, honey?" he asked Mel, hoping to drag her out of there with him. He didn't want to be apart for another second. They had a lot to talk about. "And did you manage enough photos and tweets and whatnot?" he teased.

"Yes." She grinned, but didn't miss a step in her duties as she signed forms from caterers and followed up with reporters on their way out the door and made sure everyone went home with a gift bag. "You were a very good sport, by the way."

"Does that mean I get a reward when we get home?" He ravaged her with his eyes, hoping that'd make her move a little faster.

"Absolutely."

The thought of it made him want to grab her and drag her back to the dark corner they explored the first time they visited the bar, and had him hardening behind the too-tight denim he was wearing. They needed a new topic to discuss ASAP.

"Hey babe, hand me your phone," he said.

"Why?" She eyed him suspiciously.

"I'm going to take my first selfie with my brother."

"Awww," she said. "Yes, that's a great idea. Take the photo and I'll post it. I'm just going to do one final check before we head out."

She dropped her phone in his hands, and he searched for the camera icon. He was used to his basic phone, which had maybe five icons on it, but Mel's was jacked with every app under the sun. He finally located the camera, but his big thumb got in the way and hit the wrong app, sending him to her text messages.

And that's when he saw it.

The note from Teddy.

H er little romance stunt worked well. A little too well. And now she slept in Aaron's bed, tossing and turning because he'd left the party with June.

It was innocent, she kept telling herself. Part of the plan to get them out on the town, especially after the crowd went nuts for their duet earlier in the night. There was no denying how great they sounded together. He probably decided to just go for it. Who wouldn't, given the option between the two women?

"Did you have fun?" She drove Graham home after he made out with Avery in the back alley. She had to flash the headlights twice.

He flashed her the screen on his cell, Avery's phone number glowing like the badge of honor it was.

"Nice work," she said, unable to show the enthusiasm she wanted to. She was really happy for him, and they looked absolutely adorable together. But she was still nauseous after catching Aaron sneaking out the side door with June.

"Don't worry about my brother," Graham said. "He's just out making music with June. He'll be back when they're finished."

So that's what the kids are calling it these days?

She wished she could be sure, but something told her there was more to it. She headed straight for bed after she wished Graham good night, but nothing soothed her. She stared at the ceiling mindlessly, checking the clock and her phone in fifteen minute intervals, flinching each time she heard a noise. She just wanted Aaron home in bed with her, and she didn't care how late it was, or if he was drunk. Heck, she wasn't sure she'd stay away even he had been with June. She needed him and she wasn't going to leave without a good-bye, or without touching him again.

But he never showed.

Chapter Twenty-Seven

"Mama." Mel called home the next morning when Aaron still hadn't made it home. She was exhausted, and incredibly angry that she had let herself get in the position of waiting on a man. Again. But there were things to take care of, especially once she read Teddy's message. "I just wanted to let you know that I'm going to have a more extended visit this year."

Mel had finally accomplished everything she set out to do in Atlanta. Her career was in the best shape it'd ever been in. She had respect in her office and some amazing references after Aaron's campaign. Maybe it was time to follow Frankie Fink's last piece of advice: Don't be afraid to leave to get ahead.

After what happened with Aaron, it was time to consider it.

"Sweetheart," she said, and Mel couldn't tell if she was pleased or worried. "That's not a lot of notice, but I'm sure we could pull something together. You know we'd love to have you. It's been too long. And you've heard the news?"

"Yeah, I know." She began packing up her things from the room. "It's good news. Very good. So I'm heading out this morning and we'll talk more when I get into town. I think I need to get out of the city for a while."

"Okay, baby," she said "I'll make up your room."

Most of Mel's stuff was still in storage and she could take care of that later. She'd let Aaron keep the other accessories she brought over to warm up his place. They looked good here. She knew if she took the things back now, he'd never replace them and then it'd be all cold and impersonal again, and Mel didn't want him living like that. She wanted him surrounded by nice things, in a welcoming place. She wanted that for Graham when he came back for the holidays as well. They both deserved it, so much.

And what they didn't deserve was some awkward meeting when Aaron finally made it back home. She was fine with it, really. He didn't owe her anything, and the campaign was almost over. She just had a few things to wrap up. Leaving now would make it easier on everyone.

But first she had a few calls to make.

"Where is she, Graham?" Aaron asked, when he finally made it home.

As he drove up to the apartment that morning and didn't see Mel's car in the drive, his insides hollowed and his hands went cold.

So she really decided to go to Teddy. She actually left.

After he read the text message he vowed not to mention it. She'd tell him if she wanted to. But then he said *fuck it*. He was telling her what he wanted regardless. If she walked away from him, she was going to understand exactly what she was leaving behind.

"She left," Graham signed quickly. He was obviously pissed and went to the language most comfortable for him. "Can't blame her after you took off with June last night. What was she supposed to do?"

"I told you, we were cutting a duet," he said.

"Right, and I tried to tell her that, but she didn't believe me," Graham signed.

June's manager had been so excited about their duet at the party, she wanted to capitalize on it, fast. A quick call and their labels agreed to release a single. Rita had pushed him out the door, telling him that Mel knew all about it. He should've known better than to trust her.

"She was pretty upset," Graham continued. "I like her, bro, so you better go find her and fix it."

"Jesus, Graham." He buried his head in his hands. "I love her. That's where I was after we were done—walking around the city trying to figure out what to do."

"Find her," was all Graham would say. "But take a shower first. Man, you look like hell."

As he got ready to do just that, a slam at the front door to the apartment had Aaron flying down the stairs at top speed. It wasn't Mel, of course. Like she'd coming running back to him.

It was only the mailman, who handed over a stack of envelopes. The one on top was for Mel from Teddy. He sat on the steps, turning the letter in his hands and read the return address over and over again.

Opening somebody else's mail was a crime, an invasion of property. He wouldn't do it. He couldn't.

But he wasn't going to sit around and wait. He knew what was going on here. Teddy wanted Mel back, plain and simple. And after the way he left last night, maybe she decided she wanted him, too. Fine. If that's what she wanted. But she'd damn well hear him out first. So he plugged the return address into the GPS on his phone, and he took off.

"Asshole." Aaron tried to swerve around the car ahead of him—who obviously thought it was his job to regulate traffic—without any luck. The idiot was going five miles under the speed limit, neck and neck with the car in the other lane. Meanwhile, Aaron was losing time.

According to Graham, he was about an hour behind Mel on the way to Sweetwater, and that could mean the difference between getting the girl or riding off into the sunset alone. He wasn't about to let that happen, so once a path opened up, Aaron floored it.

He had been good and pissed when he read Teddy's text on Mel's phone, not to mention hurt that she hadn't bothered to tell him about it. Sure, she'd told him the entire sorry story the first night they met, but he thought that meeting between them had already happened, and thought she had already made her decision. He'd been too busy with the launch and his career to think about anything else, which was precisely the problem.

Once he arrived at the country club, his nerves were so

frayed he could hardly speak. He wasn't the country club sort, but he'd tough it out for his girl.

Lord, he'd never stopped thinking of her that way. *His.*

Scouring the parking lot, he prayed to catch her before she could talk to Teddy.

Then he saw her, talking to some blond guy, just outside the clubhouse.

"Stop!" he yelled. "Mel don't."

She had to blink a few times because she couldn't believe her eyes. What on earth was Aaron Major doing in Sweetwater? She thought he'd be spending a lazy day in bed with June and her just-fucked hair.

She froze, while Teddy's gaze bounced back and forth between them. "Hey, that looks just like that guy. That new country singer."

"Mel," Aaron yelled again, waving his hands like a lunatic.

"Do you *know* him?" Teddy asked.

She couldn't answer his question because every cell in her body was locked on Aaron, and she couldn't move.

"Not another word," he ordered on his approach, taking Mel by the arm and leading her away from Teddy, over to the big willow tree by the clubhouse. The kissing tree, they called it. That little spot got a lot of action, because when you were under it, it seemed like the rest of the world was shut out. On a windy day, however, the branches swayed in the breeze and everyone could see what was going on. Her sister learned that the hard way during her make out session with Joe Thorton.

"I'll be right back," she called to her ex, who looked at her like she'd just sprouted another head.

She walked with Aaron, trying to find some privacy, which was nearly impossible with the entire town milling about. Well, this would get them talking. She felt the eyes of the entire town on them. Weddings were a huge event in Sweetwater, and if you were going to get married here, you better be ready to invite everyone.

This was wonderful. Once again, Melody Sharp was the center of an embarrassing scene.

"I don't understand why you're doing this, after everything we've been through," Aaron growled.

Shit, this was about the campaign. There was still a lot of wrap up, and he probably thought she'd skipped town, leaving him with nobody to finish up.

"Don't worry, you'll be fine," she said, not sure how much more she could take today. "I'll still finish up the campaign."

"What?" He shook his head, backing her into the tree. "That's all you have to say? Well, I don't really give a fuck about the campaign, Mel. That's not what this is about."

"What's it about then?" She wasn't following.

"Teddy." He sighed and she noticed how exhausted he looked. She had to stop herself from tracing the dark circles under his eyes. She prayed it wasn't because of June Skye. "And you."

"What about us?" she asked, the conversation still not making a lick of sense.

"Why don't you tell me, Mel? To my face, instead of sneaking out to be with him. You could've just told me."

Okay, there was something seriously wrong here. "Aaron," she tipped her head to meet his eyes. "I'm here to wish

Teddy luck. He's getting married. That's why he reached out to me in the first place. He wanted to be the person to tell me, so he even told my mama not to say anything. He wanted to do the right thing by me, I guess."

She had to admit, she'd been relieved to hear about Teddy. Without Aaron in the picture, it would've been too easy to say yes and come back home. But once she crossed into the city limits, she knew this place was no longer her home. It didn't suit her anymore. And more importantly, Teddy didn't suit her. Maybe he never really had. It was clear from the very first time Aaron made her blood sing. She'd never experienced that with anyone, and she'd be selling herself short if she didn't make the effort to find that kind of chemistry. Shoot, that kind of love.

"Christ, Mel." He put a hand to his heart and bent over, coming back up with a chuckle. "I thought you were coming here to get back together with him."

"What in the name of Jesus would make you think that?" She felt his head for fever. The poor man had lost his mind.

"I'm sorry. I didn't do it on purpose, but I saw the email he sent you and remembered the story and thought maybe you were still holding a torch for the guy."

She tried to absorb what he was saying, but the scene was so surreal.

"I was afraid he was going to take you from me before I even got the chance to ask you to stay." He flashed a look at Teddy that could kill.

"You came all this way to ask me to stay?"

He nodded, and her heart began to warm. "You left without saying good-bye. I jumped to all kinds of crazy conclusions."

She knew the feeling.

"So does this mean you're not with June Skye?"

"Hell no. Or yes." He reached for her hands. "I mean. I am not with June Skye."

"But you never came home…"

"We recorded a song, that's all. Rita was supposed to tell you. I was just trying to do what you wanted. I thought that if you wanted me to hang out with June, there must be a good reason. You worked so damn hard on that campaign, I wasn't going to let you down when we were so close."

"Really?" She couldn't remember a time when someone trusted her so completely.

"Really? You are so good at what you do, honey. Don't get me wrong. I wasn't thrilled about you throwing her at me. But for your publicity plan, I played along. Please don't let me chase you out of Atlanta."

"Nobody's chasing me out." Was it just her, or were people starting to close in?

"But you moved everything." Aaron looked absolutely wrecked and it was all she could do to keep her hands to herself. She'd never seen him in such a state.

"I thought maybe I was starting to cramp your style," she said, but of course the real reason was that she couldn't bear the thought of him out all night with June, or anyone else for that matter. "So I asked if I could bunk with Genn until I get back on my feet again."

"So you're not leaving the city?" Now it was Aaron moving closer.

"Not ye—" She didn't even get the words out before he pounced, lifting her to him and cutting her off with a kiss that brought her to tears. He crushed her lips, consumed them in a way that punished and rewarded her all at the same time. She would gladly take both.

"I can't believe you're here." She broke the kiss with a ragged breath. She had to look at him again because this was her dream—what she'd always wanted. Someone who knew her inside and out, and still said, *hell yes, I want you.*

"Where else would I be?" he asked, stroking her cheek. "I want you with me, Mel."

"You do?"

"Hell yes," he said. "Always." He wrapped her in his arms and they stayed that way for a long time, until she heard voices, light at first, then starting to multiply.

As predicted, the two of them began to gather quite a crowd; it was the small town way. But before she was forced to make any introductions to her people there was one thing she had to ask.

"I'm sorry," she said. "It's petty and silly, but I need to know what song you recorded with June." She braced for the answer. "It was Trophy Girl, wasn't it?"

"That matters to you?" His eyes turned a little glossy in that moment.

"It's okay." She tried to brush it off. "I'll get over it. But it was Trophy Girl? Just tell me"

"No," he whispered. "No way. I'm never recording that song."

"Why not?" she asked, both relieved and insulted. She loved that song. Her song.

"Because I'm singing it at our wedding." Then he dropped to one knee...just as she always imagined it. Just as it was supposed to be.

Acknowledgments

Wow! I can't believe I'm here celebrating my second Brazen book! Thanks to all of the readers who LOVE Brazens as much as I do, and are so enthusiastic with their support. It means the world to me. Thank you, thank you, thank, you!

Next, I have to bow down to my editor, Vanessa Mitchell. She seriously ups my game every time and will do whatever it takes to get those words out of my head and onto the page. I've been so lucky to have her.

I'm also so grateful to the entire Entangled family—I can't list them all, because there are so many working behind the scenes—but they are so dedicated to bringing amazing books to readers and it's been a wonderful experience working with them.

A big hug to Heather Howland who created the most amazing cover for PLAYED!

Once again, thanks to Danielle and Cameron at Barclay

Publicity—class-act ladies who I'm proud to have on my team. And to all the bloggers and reviewers who continually share their love of books. I appreciate all you do!

And with acknowledgements also comes a big apology to my friends and family who put up with crazy deadlines and missed dinners, and tons of other crap—I love you!

About the Author

A fan of spunky women, gorgeous guys, and super-hot romance, Clare James spends most of her time lost in books. When she's not reading, you can find her locked away writing her own steamy stories.

Clare is also a former dancer and still loves to get her groove on—mostly to work off her beloved cupcakes and red wine. She lives in Minneapolis with her two leading men—her husband and young son—and is always on social media chatting with readers.

Find her at:
www.clarejamesbooks.com
@clarejamesbooks
http://www.facebook.com/clarejamesauthor